PENGUIN BOOKS

A GUIDED TOUR THROUGH THE MUSEUM OF COMMUNISM

SLAVENKA DRAKULIĆ was born in Croatia in 1949. Her nonfiction books include *How We Survived Communism and Even Laughed*, a feminist critique of Communism that brought her to the attention of the public in the West; *The Balkan Express: Fragments from the Other Side of W—*  ess account of the war in her homeland n-guin); and *They Would Never Hurt* or of the novels *Holograms of Fear*, wh s short-listed for The Best Foreign B e *Marble Skin*, *The Taste of a Man* (Pe guin). A writer and journalist who ork Times, *The New Republic*, *The New Book Review*, and *The Nation* (where she is a contributing editor), as well as many other European magazines and newspapers, she now lives in Sweden and Croatia.

Advance Praise for
A Guided Tour Through the Museum of Communism

"Orwell taught us in *Animal Farm* that a satirical fable could introduce us to Stalinism. For our own postcommunist age, Slavenka Drakulić summons her own group of animals, each with its own literary genre, and each with a story to tell about life in a communist country. The mouse and the mole, the pig and the parrot, the raven and the bear, the cat and the dog, all seek and find ways to remind us of a time and place, and so teach us the difference between stale commemoration of the graying past and the warmth and wetness and dread and darkness of life truly and bravely recalled. This daring triumph of literary style transforms a receding epoch into the eternal present, beautifully rendering the dilemmas of life under communism as sharp instances of moral tragedy and poignant examples of the limits of self-knowledge. Literature here is an aide de memoire, not just of historical experience, but of why we choose to forget."

—Timothy Snyder, author of *Bloodlands: Europe Between Hitler and Stalin*

Praise for *Café Europa: Life After Communism*

"Profound and often bitingly funny . . . you'll never think about capitalism, modern history, or your perfect, white, American teeth in the same way again."
—*Elle*

"Insightful . . . *Café Europa* not only helps to illuminate the political and social problems facing most of Eastern Europe, but also sheds new light on the daily life of its residents, their emotional habits, fears, and dreams. . . . Moving and eloquent."
—*The New York Times*

"Where less sensitive observers might only bemoan the legacy of communism, Drakulić knows her people well and sees the redeeming nature of all their human frailty; for their sake, we should read her book."
—*San Francisco Chronicle*

"An important and timely book that deserves the widest possible audience."
—*Chicago Tribune*

Praise for *They Would Never Hurt a Fly*

"In this powerful series of reports from The Hague's international courtroom, Slavenka Drakulić confronts the Yugoslav war's grand villains and banal perpetrators as she fearlessly contemplates both the individual character of evil and the tragic, chillingly impersonal mechanisms of war. Writing with her hallmark blend of forthrightness, open-eyed irony, and psychological discernment, Drakulić gives us disturbingly intimate vignettes of war criminals who might have been her own (and our) neighbors, even as she illuminates one of our time's most daunting and urgent questions: How ordinary men and women turn, and are turned, into genocidal killers. An important and a necessary book."
—Eva Hoffman, author of *Lost in Translation* and *After Such Knowledge*

"In the first in-depth look at the war crimes trials in The Hague, Slavenka Drakulić has written a deeply personal and lucid account. She brings to life the men who destroyed Yugoslavia—mediocre people who committed extraordinary crimes."
—Laura Silber, coauthor of *Yugoslavia: Death of a Nation*

"Lucidly written . . . a devastating book . . . [Drakulić's] direct, personal style does justice to the weight and grimness of these stories."
—*The Guardian* (London)

A GUIDED TOUR THROUGH THE MUSEUM OF COMMUNISM

FABLES FROM
A MOUSE,
A PARROT,
A BEAR,
A CAT,
A MOLE,
A PIG,
A DOG,
AND A RAVEN

SLAVENKA DRAKULIĆ

PENGUIN BOOKS

PENGUIN BOOKS

Published by the Penguin Group

Penguin Group (USA) Inc., 375 Hudson Street, New York, New York 10014, U.S.A. • Penguin Group (Canada), 90 Eglinton Avenue East, Suite 700, Toronto, Ontario, Canada M4P 2Y3 (a division of Pearson Penguin Canada Inc.) • Penguin Books Ltd, 80 Strand, London WC2R 0RL, England • Penguin Ireland, 25 St Stephen's Green, Dublin 2, Ireland (a division of Penguin Books Ltd) • Penguin Group (Australia), 250 Camberwell Road, Camberwell, Victoria 3124, Australia (a division of Pearson Australia Group Pty Ltd) • Penguin Books India Pvt Ltd, 11 Community Centre, Panchsheel Park, New Delhi - 110 017, India • Penguin Group (NZ), 67 Apollo Drive, Rosedale, North Shore 0632, New Zealand (a division of Pearson New Zealand Ltd) • Penguin Books (South Africa) (Pty) Ltd, 24 Sturdee Avenue, Rosebank, Johannesburg 2196, South Africa

Penguin Books Ltd, Registered Offices:
80 Strand, London WC2R 0RL, England

First published in Penguin Books 2011

1   3   5   7   9   10   8   6   4   2

Grateful acknowledgment is made for permission to reprint "A Guided Tour Through the Museum of Communism," "The Cat-Keeper in Warsaw" and "An Interview with the Oldest Dog in Bucharest" from *Two Underdogs and a Cat* by Slavenka Drakulić. Copyright © Slavenka Drakulić, 2009. Reprinted by arrangement with Seagull Books London Limited.

PUBLISHER'S NOTE

This is a work of fiction. Names, characters, places, and incidents either are the product of the author's imagination or are used fictitiously, and any resemblance to actual persons, living or dead, business establishments, events, or locales is entirely coincidental.

LIBRARY OF CONGRESS CATALOGING IN PUBLICATION DATA

Drakulić, Slavenka, 1949–
A guided tour through the museum of communism : fables from a mouse, a parrot, a bear, a cat, a mole, a pig, a dog, and a raven / Slavenka Drakulić.
p. cm.
ISBN 978-0-14-311863-3
1. Communism—Europe, Eastern—Fiction.   2. Post-Communism—Europe, Eastern—Fiction.   3. Animals—Fiction.   4. Satire.   I. Title.
PS3554.R2375G85   2011
813'.54—dc22   2010038778

Printed in the United States of America
Set in Apollo MT   •   Designed by Elke Sigal

In memory of my long-gone canine friends,
Poli, Kiki, and Charlie

Who controls the past controls the future.
Who controls the present controls the past.

—GEORGE ORWELL

CONTENTS

ACKNOWLEDGMENTS

I would like to thank the Fischer Foundation in Germany for their generous grant, which enabled me to work on this book. My thanks to the IWM—the Institute for Human Sciences in Vienna, and to their anonymous friend who financed my Milena Jesenská grant in 2008.

Special thanks for her help with the U.S. edition to Professor Marci Shore from Yale University, to Janos M. Kovacs from IWM for his help with the Hungarian story, to my Albanian colleague, writer Bashkim Shehu, for helping me with the story about Albania, and to Claudia Ciobanu, for her help with the Romanian story.

I am grateful to Rujana for her inspiration, to Andi for his enthusiasm and to Richard for his improvements—as well as to my dear friends for their trust and support.

A SHORT NOTE TO THE READER

I am aware that, if you are not familiar with Eastern Europe under Communism, some stories from this book might appear to you highly fictitious, if not outright fantasy. Therefore, I would like to assure you that, unfortunately, this is not the case. From the point of view of persons and events described, regardless of whether a story is narrated by a dog, a cat, or some other domestic, wild, or exotic animal, it all really happened. This is easy enough to check. Indeed, as a fiction writer I often felt shamed by the imagination of politicians, of which there is ample proof in this book!

However, writing again and again about the rule of Communism and its consequences for ordinary people, I came to the conclusion that we did not have "too much history," as it is often said about this part of the world. Rather, we had too much memory and too many myths. And, in my life experience, this is a dangerous combination that has often resulted in ideology and manipulation leading to conflict and terrible suffering.

I

A GUIDED TOUR THROUGH THE MUSEUM OF COMMUNISM

Come in, come in, please! Don't worry, this is only a *museum* of Communism, not the real thing!

I am joking. But do come in, please. You are Hans, from Würzburg, I presume? I was expecting you. I am Bohumil, your distant relative. I live in this Prague museum in a school cabinet, among the old textbooks. It suits me. I am a bookish type, a book mouse, one could say, ha-ha! Some time ago my grammar school became a private university and the classrooms were refurbished. My cabinet was thrown out. I thought that would be the end of my comfortable life. But luckily, some people from the museum came along and brought the cabinet here, as an exhibit from the old times.

I share my days with Milena, an elderly cleaning woman who also sells souvenirs in the museum shop. She pretends that she doesn't know that I live here. But why then, I ask you, did she try to kill me with her broom the very first time she saw me, an ordinary little mouse? Well, not kill perhaps, but scare me off. As I had no other place to go, she reconciled herself to my existence. Perhaps she thought that, after all, I am an underdog just like her? Now she leaves crumbs of bread and pieces of apple and cheese near my cabinet every evening before she leaves. Often, when we are alone, she is talking to me. She calls me Bohumil! She says, "You know, Bohumil, what happened to me today?"—and then goes on with her story. I usually stand on the windowsill and listen to her, keep her company. It took me some time to understand that since there is nobody around, Bohumil is—well, me!

She went out to smoke a cigarette now; she won't be back for a while. The only thing I hold against Milena is that she's a heavy smoker, even though it's bad for her health. And for mine, too. In fact, I discovered that I have an allergy to cigarettes. Although she often opens a window to the courtyard to let out the smelly air. It's an old habit from when she used to work in the state archive as a secretary. Not as a cleaner, mind you. Milena studied English and French. Speaking of air, she says that any institution that has anything to do with the Communist state, even this one, smells of dust. Perhaps from too many papers, documents about God knows what and God knows whom . . . Milena used to worry, you know, if her husband was registered in the files of the secret police. Of course he was registered! Like, he was a "security risk"! *"Any state that has to depend on police reports about citizens like him, just an ordinary engineer in an electrical plant, is pathetic!,"* she used to say to her friend Dáša, a cleaning woman from the casino downstairs. But obviously, this is how it was; every citizen was considered to be a "security risk" back then. However, in the new democracy, because of so-called *privatization*, her Marek lost his job. That's why she works here; they need the money.

I cannot say that I mind living in this museum, although it was really more interesting living in the grammar school. I learned a lot about Communism by listening to the lectures of a history teacher there. Perlík was his name. I heard that he was also a poet, a kind of dissident intellectual, and that he even spent some time in jail when he was young.

You don't have such a museum in Würzburg, you say, and your knowledge of Communism is almost nonexistent. Well, since you are here in Prague as a tourist, I could show you around. I consider myself qualified to be a guide here, but the sad truth is that the museum would not employ a mouse. I can tell you that the more time I spend here, the more I realize how important this museum is. I remember Professor Perlík's words that the time would soon come when kids would say: Communism, what's *that*? A religion? A maker of cars perhaps? And from what I heard from him, this is simply not right, Communism shouldn't be remembered just by the likes of the professor or Milena, who survived it. It should be remembered for its bad sides and good; there must have been something good one can say about it, although that's not a popular view to hold these days, I gather. For example, people could get a solid education, they say. Or there's the fact that the Communist USSR fought against the Nazis in the Second World War. Yet Milena says that watching Hollywood movies one gets the impression that it was the Americans who won it all on their own!

No, life under Communism should not be forgotten, although that is exactly what I see happening. In this museum shop, by the way, you can buy a history book about the dark past for only five euros. It's cheap. And it is only a hundred pages long, in large print. "The older I get, the more I appreciate it," says Milena. You can read here, for example (I heard someone reading it with my own ears!), that the wife of President Klement Gottwald was rather fat, or that the wife of Antonín Novotný (the man who later became president himself) took the china and the bedsheets from the flat of Vladimír Clementis. Of course, only after he was executed in the purges of the fifties. You can also learn—as I did—that 257,964 people sentenced for political reasons were rehabilitated in 1990.

Some visitors don't care at all about such facts; they just purchase posters, stamps, T-shirts, and USSR military caps, along with wax candles in the forms of Stalin, Marx, and Lenin. These are the single most popular souvenirs sold in the shop, I can tell you, maybe because they are the cheapest. I admit that I can hardly imagine the excitement of a person watching Stalin slowly melt down into a puddle of wax, but there are buyers who enjoy such symbolic acts.

As you come in, you inevitably notice busts and statues of Marx, Lenin, Stalin. A young man, a Czech, was here recently. Looking at Marx, he said: "Is that some Orthodox priest?" You could say that Marx, with his beard, did indeed look like one. You could also say that he was rather orthodox in his views and, in some ways, even like a priest, preaching his doctrine. But even I was astonished by the young man's ignorance. What would Professor Perlík have made of his question? He would wonder what they teach them in history class nowadays, and would probably tell the boy, Well, read about him, you *durak*! That means stupid in Russian, but they don't teach them Russian anymore. It is sad, although understandable. From my limited perspective as a mouse, a language is a language. It is worth learning regardless of the historical circumstances, no? But what can such an ignorant person read here in the museum about a historical figure like Karl Marx and the origins of Communism? See, here it says that he was "a bohemian and an intellectual adventurer, who started his career as a romantic poet with an inclination toward apocalyptic titanism, a sharp-tongued journalist"—as if that would somehow disqualify him from writing *Das Kapital*! Or look at this text about Lenin: "From the very beginning, Lenin pushed for the tactics of extreme perfidiousness and ruthlessness which became characteristic of all Communist regimes of the time." What can I tell you? I know from Professor Perlík's lectures that in Communist times, Lenin was glorified much too much, and that textbooks were even more seasoned with such descriptions and with the same kind of cheap psychology as this one! But the professor would probably say that there is no need for ideology nowadays and that we need history instead.

You know, sometimes when they come to this room with paintings from the Soviet school of socialist realism, with busts and a spaceship and a school class and a workshop—all in one room!—I can see how disappointed visitors are. I peek out at them from my cabinet, and our visitors look to me like those people who love to visit freak shows with a two-headed goat or a bearded woman—that kind of thing. Of course, I see why they are disappointed—there is no Stalin in a cage, not even a mummy of Lenin! They see only a heap of old things here, more like a junkyard, which in fact it is. Exhibits here are from flea markets and all kinds of garage sales, even straight out of rubbish bins. See, here Communism is finally reduced to the rubbish heap of history! Isn't that what the velvet revolution in 1989 was all about? That is what I would like to tell them when they make faces, like, Is that *all* you have here? What more would they want to *see*?

Permit me to say that, from what I have heard from the professor, Communism is not so much about exhibits, about *seeing*. It is more about how one lived in those times, or more to the point, how one survived them. From the lack of food or shoes to the lack of freedom and human rights. The question is, How do you present that kind of shortage, shortages that were not just poverty-induced, to somebody who knows very little about it? Because people who experienced life under Communism tend not to come here, anyway. I am afraid that our Innocent Visitor, as I call such people, has to use his imagination. Therefore, I sometimes think that Milena is the best "exhibit" they could see here, because she lived most of her life under Communism. If only visitors would ask her about her life . . . but nobody does.

Let me first tell you about the museum itself, advertised as "above McDonald's, next to the Casino." Indeed, it is very properly situated in Na Přikope, "*in the heart of consumer capitalism*," as one visitor remarked the other day. It was opened in December of 2001 in the nineteenth-century Palác Savarin. It stores roughly one thousand artifacts in four rooms and was founded privately by an American of Czech origin. Why was it privately funded? Excellent question, Hans, and very logical too! Because, astonishingly enough, nobody from the democratic government hit upon this idea. Strange, you may think, that such an important era of the recent past would not have been documented had it not been for a couple of enthusiasts. You think the reason might be that it deals with too painful a time, that memories are still too vivid? Well, I wonder about that. If you ask Milena, there is another reason why the Czechs (or Slovaks, for that matter; this is their museum, too!) don't care about such a museum and don't visit it either. *"They want to run as far away from Communism as they can.* Our young people don't care, for them Communism is the ancient past. Those old enough to remember it want to forget it now. And why? *Because they went along with it.* As I did. As my husband did, and our neighbors, and everybody we knew, every Pavel and Elena around us," I heard her say.

I remember that I once heard Professor Perlík say that today everybody claims they were not members of the Communist Party, that they did not really belong. "If you believed what people here say, you would think that *not a single person* in this whole country was ever a member of the Communist Party of Czechoslovakia! *They all were victims!* That is rather stupid, especially given the fact that *10 percent* of the population were party members, plain and simple. That means *one million seven hundred thousand people*! I understand that not all of them were believers; they were only formally members because of the job and career and benefits that went with membership. But no regime, however totalitarian, could exist without complicity on the part of the people—however unwilling it might be," I remember Professor Perlík saying. "Let us not kid ourselves; most of us complied in order not only to survive—because Czecho-slovakia was not the USSR—but just to live better. I admit it's a hard fact to face now. But yes, there is a difference between those who were members only formally and those who really collaborated. Perhaps it sounds to you as if there is no big difference between the two? Collaboration is a more active attitude, a kind of partnership. For example, while most ordinary members of the party merely complied, some collaborated with the regime. "There are many shades of gray," he used to say. And then he quoted Vaclav Havel, the hero of the "velvet revolution," who himself said that the line between victim and oppressor runs de facto through each person, for everyone in his or her own way is both a victim and a supporter of the system.

I realized that it is not without reason that the history of the CPCz, the Communist Party of Czechoslovakia, is written on a single long scroll of paper, glued to the wall, almost as if intended not to be seen. I guess what I am trying to explain to you here is that I learned how the most important things about Communism are the invisible ones. And that in this museum you won't see *the shades of gray* that prevailed in everyday life. That is why such a museum *reaches only so deep*—this criticism comes from a very learned man who was here, maybe a curator in another museum, or some kind of critic. According to him, the museum does not—and cannot—show you the full depth of what people lived through. "There is no personal history given here, no individual destiny," the man said. On the other hand, perhaps no museum of Communism is capable of doing that. And you know what I think? Not that the opinion of someone like me counts at all, but nevertheless I'll tell you that maybe this museum got it right! Maybe the absence of individual stories is the best illustration of the fact that individualism was the biggest sin one could commit.

Ah, but I am getting too pedagogical, I'm afraid! My dear Hans, you must tell me if I am treating you like a total ignorant, you must stop me if I am boring you! I guess my attitude comes from the fact that too many Americans pass the museum nowadays . . .

But you are telling me to go on? Okay then, where was I? Yes, I wanted to say that Communist regimes generally seemed to prefer numbers over stories. Numbers are abstract, they create a kind of "scientific" neutrality. Let me give you an example, used by Professor Perlík: In his history class I heard him tell his pupils that Hitler exterminated some six million Jews in Europe during the Second World War. They gave him a blank look and continued to chat, and to push and throw things at each other. The information didn't even catch their attention—let alone their imaginations. But then, he took his class to Poland. They visited Auschwitz death camps. I remember them talking afterward about that visit, about how memorable that spring day had been for them. Of course, Professor Perlík had already told them before what had happened there, but still they were totally unprepared. Evidently, nothing can prepare you for such horror—and that is kind of good, he said. You grasp the horror better once you see, with your own eyes, heaps of human hair, shoes, glasses . . . heaps of them. All that, every item, belonged to an individual with a name, to a real live person. He also told them that during Communism, he could not have told his pupils that some thirty million people died in the labor camps in Siberia. It was taboo. But I suspect that the professor told them just that, landing himself in prison.

Now, let's go back to what you actually see here—what you see here is only a pile of dusty things, like in an old antique shop or a flea market somewhere in Kosice (though I've never been there, I heard someone making this comparison). Therefore, it seems that it is more important to see the invisible yet omnipresent ugliness of the Communist mentality, of which the artifacts in this museum are just a reflection. By mentality, I mean a certain way of thinking and behaving that developed over decades under harsh conditions. Not solidarity, as you might expect of people living under duress, but its opposite, selfishness, a *slow hardening of the soul* (this formulation, you rightly guess, comes from the more poetic side of our professor). Yet, only art, especially literature, can show you that. Novels like those of a certain Milan Kundera, a writer whose name I have often heard mentioned in this museum of late.

Our visitors usually want to take photos in this particular room. For example, if they stand here, where I am standing, they can take a photo of this beautiful nineteenth-century crystal chandelier hanging from the ceiling. Indeed, they can get it in the same frame as the hammer and sickle—a really nice souvenir! By the way, this chandelier is widely considered by our visitors to be the only beautiful item in here. Although not intended as an exhibit, you could still say—as I have heard here—that it symbolizes the life of the bourgeoisie, the class enemy. As does this whole spacious apartment. "Look, a beautiful bourgeois apartment full of ugly things produced during Communism!" someone exclaimed recently.

I kind of like the fact that this is a museum of ugly things. By the time visitors like you arrive here, they have had their fill of the beautiful buildings in the neighborhood, so they don't notice beauty any longer. Golden altars, baroque facades, angels, Madonnas, spectacular church paintings . . . Indeed, I have seen such things myself during my excursions into the neighborhood. Here, in this museum, like in real Communism, ugliness reigns. Sometimes I hear foreigners wonder aloud: "Why doesn't Communism care about beauty?" You only need to go to the southern outskirts of Prague to see whole blocks of ghastly gray housing developments, called "*paneláky*" because they were built out of prefabricated material in the seventies. By the way, that material is great for us mice; it is so easy to make a nice home there! Yet, these buildings provided a home for millions of people (and mice)—for the so-called proletariat!—who moved from their villages to the city to work in industry. Milena and her Marek still live in such a building, in a two-room 63-square-meter apartment. They were happy when they got it in the sixties, after years of waiting in a single rented room heated by a coal-burning stove instead of an electric one or a central heating system.

Almost anything that was produced under Communism anywhere—from apartment buildings to clothes, from furniture to pots and pans—is considered to be ugly. Although this was not the case in this very country, the Communist system originally was built by and for poor peasants. Where would they get a sense of beauty? Functionality, not looks, was the priority in every aspect, the arts included; hence socialist realism, of course. Any divergence from that rule, say, abstract painting, was simply punished and forbidden—in the USSR after the thirties, for example. Art in general—painting, for instance—had a political-ideological-educational role, much as did medieval frescoes that explained the beginning of the world (and religion) to the masses. Ugliness was built into that system, I learned from Jana Strugalová, who taught art in our grammar school and was herself very beautiful. Some examples you see exhibited here, like the furniture in this "typical living room" (Soviet) where we are standing now. "Style of living," it says. As if poverty were a "style"! Style is something one chooses; even a mouse can understand that . . .

Now, if you take a look at the representation of a typical school classroom to your right, what do you see? A blackboard, a few benches, and a cabinet—that's where I live, by the way. It doesn't tell you much, except for, perhaps, one detail. Have you noticed that the textbooks and the writing on the blackboard are in the Cyrillic alphabet? No? The Czech alphabet uses the Latin script. This exhibit obviously symbolizes a Soviet classroom. You must have noticed that the majority of objects exhibited so far have to do with the Soviet Union, not Czechoslovakia, as the country was called before the split in 1993. If you pay attention to the details, it is easy to conclude that the USSR is overrepresented in this museum, as one visitor observed. We are in Prague, after all, but all visitors get (as you yourself can witness) is a kind of written chronology of the Czechoslovak Communist Party in that corridor that you passed. This clearly suggests that Czechs see themselves as the victims of Communism, not as the "original sinners," so to speak. Later you will see, when we come to 1968, that the rebellion against the Soviet occupation is much better documented. The rebellion is important, something to be proud of, therefore there are a lot of photos and even documentary films. As if the creators of this museum (but we are not supposed to bite the hand that feeds us, as Milena would say!) were a bit ashamed of Czech history, of the fact that, say, in the elections of 1946 some 40 percent of the people voted for the Communists. You'll agree that the Czechs can't blame the USSR for that!

Milena says that her family, like millions of others, was responsible for accepting the new political system. Theirs is by no means an exceptional story; nobody was jailed, murdered, or tortured. Her parents came here after the war from some Bohemian village and got a job in a furniture factory, happy to put their hard life on the land behind them. She and her brother (I saw him when he visited Milena here) went to a grammar school. Their parents insisted that they study because that was the only way to a better life, they believed. They were right. The brother became a doctor. Milena began studying foreign languages soon after she'd met her husband. He was a student of electrical engineering. When the baby came, someone had to work, and that someone was Milena. They both tried to stay out of politics, accepting party membership because it was the obvious way to get an apartment, a car, a vacation in Bulgaria. In hindsight, she admits, they were passive, meek, and submissive. A bit like us mice, you know . . . It was the only way if you were not prepared to go to jail, and we would like to forget that now.

Let's stop at this exhibit of a typical shop in the USSR. Shops here looked much better, so I was made to understand. In comparison to Moscow, Prague shops were like elegant supermarkets: full of food, especially after 1968, in the period of so-called normalization. Here you could see two kinds of canned food. That's perhaps an exaggeration; there must have been a few more items in the shops in the USSR, at least in the big cities. Still, you have to imagine what it was like to live on very meager means. Ordinary poverty, you think? I've heard others say that too, meaning that there was poverty in the West also, especially after the war. Well, you could call it poverty, I suppose, but it is really not the same. "Poverty is when there are things to buy but you don't have the money for them. A shortage is something else: it is when you have the money but there is nothing to buy—the articles are either not produced or not delivered to the shops—because of the way the planned economy works." Again, this is how Professor Perlík explained it to his pupils. "I mean, you had to be very skillful to get certain products, like shoes, for example. It worked almost like the natural exchange of goods, or if not goods, then services: If you provide me with the medicine I need, I can help you get a better coat, and so forth," he explained.

Also, shortages seem to be the key to understanding the end of Communism. You think it was Pope John Paul II? Or Mikhail Gorbachev's ideas of glasnost and perestroika? Or both of them combined? Yes, of course, everybody agrees on that. But take a look at this shop again. Toilet paper is not exhibited here, and for good reason: There wasn't any. Nor were there sanitary napkins, or diapers, or washing powder—not to mention coffee, butter, or oranges. Milena remembers when a friend would travel abroad— Yugoslavia was abroad then, because it was outside of the Soviet bloc—and there in the midseventies you could get toilet paper— her friend would fill a suitcase with rolls and rolls of it! Banalities, you might say—but they, too, decided the destiny of the Communist regimes everywhere. In order to understand why Communism failed, one has to know that it could not produce the basic things people needed. Or, perhaps, not enough of them. How long could such regimes last? The success of a political system is also measured in terms of the goods available to ordinary people, I suppose. And to mice, I might add. Sometimes, when I am making my bed from the fine, soft Italian toilet paper that Milena puts in our toilets, I wonder if my life would have been different if I had been born under Communism. Yet, there is communism and Communism, of course. My cousins in Romania, for example, had to chew on their tails sometimes just to keep hunger at bay. That was never the case here. In Czechoslovakia during Communism, the authorities merely needed to keep the price of beer low; otherwise they would have had a real revolution on their hands! Most probably that was the main reason why beer was always so cheap here.

Now we come to an interrogation room. Everybody says that this is the centerpiece of this museum. Indeed, here you can see what I mean when I keep saying that in this museum much is left to the individual imagination. Again, there is not much for you to actually see in this room: a desk, two chairs—one in front, one behind the desk—a lamp, an old typewriter, a hanger with the notorious black leather coat. Why notorious? Because they say that agents of the Soviet secret police would come for you in the middle of the night habitually wearing such a coat. Yet, what can these *things*, this setting, tell visitors like you, if you don't know what happened in such interrogation rooms? Not much. You can see the statistics on the wall—names and numbers, again. They hide horrible stories, but as in the case of Auschwitz, these are abstractions. How can one present the people, the living persons behind the numbers? You have to make an effort to see the individual destiny, a man who has been interrogated and whose spirit is broken. Professor Perlík mentioned Arthur Koestler's book *Darkness at Noon* and Arthur London's *The Confession*—if I remember correctly. I know that the professor had a neighbor who testified at the trial of Rudolf Slansky during the first wave of Stalinist purges in the fifties here. He survived the whole ordeal. "But that man," said the professor nodding sadly, "was never the same again."

If anything, this room is the symbol of absolute power. In such rooms they would force people to betray not only others but themselves as well. On the other hand, this was the destiny of relatively few people. But think of something else not represented here. Think of how people lived—hundreds of millions of them—with a feeling that an interrogation room had been installed in their brains. You could not see it, but it was there.

Now again you might think that I am exaggerating. But I'm merely speaking of *self-censorship*. It is a situation in which you yourself become your own interrogator—on exactly the opposite side of freedom of expression. What, you wonder if this was a form of political correctness? My dear Hans . . . let me put it this way, if I might quote the professor again: "Political correctness grew out of a concern for others; self-censorship grew out of a fear of others." Surveillance of each other was installed as a system—perfected in the USSR but practiced everywhere. For example, you had no way of knowing if your elderly neighbor, who would even cook you a soup when you were ill, was in fact reporting on your every word and move. If you could not trust the people around you, in your house or at work, you would behave cautiously, controlling yourself. The system of surveillance and self-control lives off of fear and suspicion. It is a simple and efficient psychological mechanism that turns people into liars—and, therefore, into accomplices of the regime.

But, again, there were *shades of gray* even within this self-censorship. Antonín Novotný was not exactly Stalin, even if there are those who would like to see him like that nowadays. He used to blow his top over films like *Closely Watched Trains* by Jirí Menzel, which was awarded an Oscar in 1967, and *The Firemen's Ball*, By Milos Forman. Or over novels by Ludvik Vaculik, Pavel Kohout, and Milan Kundera, all critical of Communism. In the midsixties the atmosphere in this country became so liberal that Secretary General Alexander Dubček believed it was even possible to reform Communism when he became secretary general in 1967. The invasion by the Warsaw Pact military force in 1968 started because of the Soviet fear of our reforms—of losing its grip on us, that is.

I recently overheard Milena telling some visitors the following story:

"That summer I saw Soviet tanks rolling into the streets of Prague. I will never forget that day. I was barely twenty years old, and I had gone out with my brother. We were running some errands downtown, and at one moment he asked me to buy him an ice cream. It was August twenty-first, a pleasant, sunny morning. We were somewhere near the National Theatre, and there, at the corner, was an ice cream stand. And just as we were turning to get there we heard a strange noise. It sounded like a thunderstorm at first, then like some huge, powerful machine moving. Indeed, I felt the asphalt tremble under my feet. As we were about to cross the road, we saw a tank at the bottom of the street, some hundred meters away. A tank in the middle of Prague! I had never seen a real one before, only in war movies. It was slowly coming toward us, very slowly, as if the soldiers were in no particular hurry. I remember we both just stood there, looking, as if hypnotized . . .

"Here, you see this photo? It was taken on the morning of August 21, 1968, by the Hajný brothers, Jan and Bohumil. Their photos became famous later. You see that woman with the small boy? Well, that happens to be me. Do you notice something odd about this photo? See how the people are behaving; see the woman with the white handbag. She must have heard the tank; she must have seen it coming. Yet she is walking down the street as if taking a stroll, probably deliberately so. Nobody seems to be panicking in this picture, and that, considering that the tanks are rolling closer and closer, is very strange behavior, no? You would think that people would be screaming and running away, scared. But no, the citizens of Prague are slowly walking, minding their own business, while the occupation army is entering their city! Oh, I just love this photo! No, not because I am in it, but because it captures a certain attitude of the people: pride, arrogance, even, in the face of might—like a kind of highly civilized act of protest. A kind of heroism the Czech way, as if we were saying, we are superior to your tanks. That is how we were, proud, brave. Those tanks did not humiliate us. We felt undefeated—at least for a short while! The best of Czechoslovakia is here in these photos. When you think that it was not about a revolution, not a demand to abolish Communism, but only to reform it into 'socialism with a human face.' . . . That day we listened to radio reports about what was happening, about clashes with the tanks in Vinohradska Street. The people of Prague were fighting the Warsaw Pact's 750,000 troops and 6,000 tanks with Molotov cocktails and barricades! We had no chance. Dubček was kidnapped by the KGB and forced to sign the Moscow Protocol that legalized the Soviet occupation. I still remember that feeling of powerlessness and defeat that settled in and stayed with us for the next twenty years."

"At least people now know that 1968 in Czechoslovakia was the beginning of the end," the professor used to say. "They learned the hard way that Communism is not to be reformed. But never in their wildest dreams could they have imagined that another attempt to reform Communism—a copy of 1968!—

would come from within the USSR itself, and that it would mean its demise. Did you know that Gorbachev was friends with Zdeněk Mlynář, one of the leading figures of the Prague spring? Ah, Gorby, hated and forgotten in his own country . . . I remember how the whole Western world applauded him, as if he really wanted to dispatch Communism to the 'graveyard of history,' as it were. His achievement was that he did not, could not, send the army against us again (or against other Communist countries, for that matter). And this made it possible for our revolution to be velvet. Not so velvet as one might think, though: My own son, a student then, got hit in the head by the police during the November seventeenth student protest. My daughter soon became a member of Obcanske forum and knew Vaclav Havel personally. To me it's as if it all happened yesterday . . . Yet, it was twenty years ago when I was standing under the balcony at Vaclavske namesti, where Havel was speaking, and chanting: *'Havel to the castle!'* We wanted him to become president, and imagine—he did! He did! But once the dream was fulfilled, reality sank in."

Here in the museum we have a cinema where you could, if you had the time, see documentary films about the revolution. The velvet revolution is a well-documented event; even you, Hans, have heard of it. This perhaps is the reason why not that many visitors sit here and watch—they have already seen it somewhere. And here, in this cinema, is the end of the story about Communism. In the museum, I mean.

"What did the change bring me?" Milena says. "I've lost my job. I have less money. My husband drinks. Freedom? What freedom? We can't travel anywhere, we can't buy things. We don't even have a car now, can't afford to keep it," she laments to Dáša, who can only share her feeling. I sometimes feel sorry for both of them; they are obviously among the losers. These two ladies are perhaps not the best advertisement for democracy and capitalism, I'd say. The change happened too late for them. Indeed, what a frustration it must be to finally live in an age of plenty but not to be able to enjoy it, don't you think, Hans?

It seems to me, judging from the little knowledge I acquired as a mouse in the Museum of Communism, that this frustration might be the reason why there is still something mean and suspicious, something hypocritical in people. Vestiges of former times, I suppose. As if people haven't changed *that* much, not in their minds. I will give you an example: Earlier I mentioned Milan Kundera. He is allegedly the most famous Czech writer; you might even have seen a film made in Hollywood adapted from his novel *The Unbearable Lightness of Being*? You know him? Well then, you also know that all his early novels deal with Communist repression in his country, like *The Joke*. In that book, Ludvik ends up in a labor camp, in a mine, just because he wrote a postcard to a former girlfriend: "Optimism is the opium of the masses! A healthy atmosphere stinks of stupidity! Long live Trotsky!" He meant it as a joke, but the police judged it as political text. Kundera left Czechoslovakia and went to France after the invasion in 1968 and never returned. After that he became one of the best-known dissidents from the Communist world, next to Alexander Solzhenitsyn.

Suddenly, this same Kundera is in the middle of a scandal! I heard about it from a couple discussing it very loudly in this room just recently. In fact, they woke me up in the middle of my regular afternoon nap. What happened? In October 2008 a certain historian found a document that is taken as proof that Kundera is not what he seems to be. Not a moral man, but a *denouncer* no less. A document from 1950 is there to prove it. It is a police report, a short one. It states that Milan Kundera, at that time a student at the FAMU film academy and an ardent member of the CP, reported to the undersigned police inspector that there was a suspicious person staying in his dormitory. Following this, the police arrested Miroslav Dvoraček, a pilot and a spy for the American-supported Czech intelligence agency of that time. Dvoraček had illegally crossed the border back into Czechoslovakia and was on his way out again. Following Kundera's report, the man was arrested and sentenced to twenty-two years of hard labor. Dvoraček served his sentence mostly in uranium mines. Yet, in his writing and interviews, Kundera never mentioned this episode.

"Now, again, we are seeing the resurrection of the same old pattern of suspicion that nobody is what he claims to be," I heard the woman say angrily, as if she personally had suffered the consequence of his betrayal. "A dissident is not a dissident but a fugitive from his not very honorable past; a moral person is in fact immoral. Falsehood is truth, and so on. Until yesterday you would have believed that Kundera was a symbol of morality."

"Well," the man said, rather calmly, "every normal person should ask himself, But is that report real and not a setup? How come the document was discovered only now and by what 'co-incidence'? No one believes in coincidences; there were too many of them in the past. Moreover, what's the purpose of this 'discovery' and of publishing it? In short—who benefits from it today? I tend to just dismiss such coincidences; we should know better. No, the problem lies elsewhere: You see, true or not, the real problem is that this whole devilish story is believable. Convincing. Everybody agrees that it could have happened. It could have been that Kundera saw reporting on Dvoraček as his patriotic duty: He was a party member, he himself was in danger of going to prison if he didn't report it, such were the times. It could have happened to anyone—or so the argument goes."

"But *this* is the false argument!" the woman interrupted him. "Kundera is in no way 'one *of us*,' Kundera is—well, Kundera. What about his confession, then? People say, Why doesn't he confess now, when his big secret is out? He should get it off his chest. Nonsense! They say such nonsense, in my opinion, because if such a great writer and dissident had made such a terrible denunciation then our own denunciations and compromises would look comparatively much pettier. So what if Svoboda spied on Markus and he was transferred to a worse job? At least he did not wind up in prison."

"I agree," the man said. Now his voice sounded sad. "There is a certain malevolent triumph in the 'fact' (or *the fact*, depending on how you look at it) that the best of us all could have failed. Even if it is not true but only a suspicion, only a possibility—it excites people. It makes heroes more human, petty like the rest of us. If he would only confess, they would immediately grant him forgiveness!"

"Ah, yes, forgiveness! My foot! They couldn't wait to take away his moral credibility—since they couldn't take away his talent and his fame," the woman added, even more worked up now. "But he is a stubborn old man. And he also must know that his confession would only make it easier for such people, but not for himself. In a way, all these questions are unimportant and belated, because the seed of suspicion has been planted. If he is not guilty, however hard he tries, Kundera won't be able to wash himself clean of it. If he is guilty it is sad, but it doesn't annihilate his writing. If this is some consolation to him . . . ," she concluded.

Why am I telling you about this particular case? Because—the way I understand Communism—it still belongs to the museum. Twenty years after its collapse, it illustrates the state of people's minds here.

My dear Hans, I can hear Milena coming, she will be back any moment now . . . unfortunately that means you have to go. It was nice of you to visit me. I told you, she is not scared of me, even if she is a woman, and we know how hysterical they can get when they see a mouse. But I am not sure how she would react to you; you rats are much bigger than mice. You could scare her. I have to protect her from shock, because she has a weak heart. I also have to protect myself, because who knows who would come here if she were to go? I am sure you understand what I mean.

I hope that you found the museum interesting. I am afraid that you probably find me not competent enough as a guide. But I couldn't tell how much you know about Communism and I wanted you to get a grasp of it. Remember, I am only an amateur guide! Anyway, Professor Perlík would say that what is important is what you do not see: fear, complicity, and the hypocrisy of life under Communism. However modest and superficial the museum might look to you, the importance of it is that it exists. That, in itself, is a miracle! Because, tell me, who would have ever thought, twenty years ago, that Communism would end up like this, in a museum? Or, for that matter, that you would visit me here, and that I would be your guide?

So long, and have a nice holiday in Paris!

II

A COMMUNIST WITH STYLE

And who the fuck are you? Why are you staring at Koki? Have you never seen a talking parrot before? A singing parrot? A swearing parrot? Well, then you should visit a Web site called YouTube—there are lots of parrots there. One of Koki's favorites is Menino, singing the "Queen of the Night" aria from Mozart's *Magic Flute*. Menino's performance is absolutely outstanding, Koki feels very proud as he watches him on the computer in the lobby of the hotel. But Koki also enjoys watching people watching Menino and their astonishment at seeing the green bird sing Mozart. You think that monkeys are your closest relatives. But can they sing? The hell they can! They merely shriek; that's the closest they come to it. No, we parrots are the closest to you people for at least several reasons: First, we can sing and we can talk. Besides, you people often behave like parrots yourselves, especially here, in the presence of bigwigs. You imitate us, repeating whatever any of the dignitaries say as if it were sacrosanct. It is funny to see how some people from the president's various summer entourages here in the Croation president's summer residence listen to and repeat every word, as if they believe they can benefit from it. But I guess this is how every royal household functions, with its parrots and hawks, cats and dogs, cows and sheep—the entire menagerie. Sometimes Koki entertains himself by guessing who is what in that coterie—in the "court *camarilla*" as the Marshal, the former president of the former Yugoslavia, used to say with contempt. Although, where would the Marshal himself have been without his *camarilla*?

Oh, Koki can see that you are a tourist and he can guess that you are here because of the Marshal. And you expect Koki to tell you stories about him, yes? Yes. Koki used to be part of the Marshal's zoo here on one of the fourteen islands in the Brioni archipelago that he used as his summer residence during his reign. At that time, of course, Koki did not need to entertain people like you. Oh, no! You bloody tourists could not get anywhere near this place. Koki must say that he performed for a very different kind of public then—for heads of state, aristocrats, and movie stars, no less. To give you an idea, suffice it to say that the Marshal received here Eleanor Roosevelt and Queen Elizabeth, as well as Jacqueline Kennedy, Che Guevara and Fidel Castro, Haile Selassie and Indira Gandhi, Jawaharlal Nehru and Nikita Khrushchev, Josephine Baker and Princess Margaret—not to mention Hollywood film stars! And in the times before Tito, the archipelago was visited by Archduke Franz Ferdinand and Kaiser Wilhelm II, along with aristocrats from Vienna and Budapest, Munich and Berlin. Those were the days . . .

But now, although the presidential residence is still here, and every new president comes regularly to enjoy it (that has not changed), the country has somehow shrunk, and there are not many such distinguished visitors coming here anymore. Either the last two presidents were not as fascinating as the old one, or the shrunken country is no longer very important, Koki can't tell. He only knows that, because the new shrunken country has a democracy instead of a dictatorship now, tourists can visit and stare at Koki, expecting to be entertained. Nowadays, Koki is just a tourist worker, and he makes his living by chatting in five languages. But he is not stupid! In the last twenty years Koki, too, has changed: It is one thing to be a spoiled clown—another to be a tourist attraction. Koki politely greets visitors and Koki politely swears, yes, that's true. But if they want more, Koki wants more food in return! It is called bribery, but corruption is a very popular, recognized, and even rewarded way of making your living in this new state. Ah, I see that I have to explain this: We also had corruption in the former Yugoslavia, but it was indirect; it had to do with who knew whom, while now the new, additional element is money.

So, if you feed Koki some nuts (which you are not supposed to do) he might decide to tell you a story or two. Agreed? Well, then we are all set.

You must have read a few things about the Marshal, at least in your guidebooks. There are over a thousand books written about him—too many, and not too good, I hear. And what can you read in them? That he was one of the greatest historical persons? Or perhaps a dictator in Yugoslavia, a country ruled by the Communist Party, which collapsed some twenty years ago in a spate of bloody wars? Why, you ask? Because every little nation wanted to have its own little nation-state! Imagine, if there had been more than one parrot on this island—Perhaps we, too, could have asked for independence? Terrible that these wars in the nineties took so many lives, some two hundred thousand, they say—but that is another story. As is the Marshal's historical role in all of it. About which Koki, naturally, knows too little, because he is just a little birdie.

Let Koki save you the trouble and simplify what is usually written about the Marshal in guidebooks, textbooks, history books, and the like: It is said that he was a locksmith by profession; he was born into a poor peasant family; and he ended up as a prisoner in Russia during World War I. He became a member of the Communist Party in Yugoslavia in the thirties and fought his way up—fought against fascism as commander of the partisan army, when Yugoslavia was occupied by the Germans and Italians during World War II. Afterward, he finally became president—once he had carried out a Communist revolution, of course—and, in the best tradition of such states, at the same time held the highest position in the army as well. The Marshal also founded the so-called nonaligned movement in the sixties. All these African and Arab countries, offended by their colonizers, they loved him, yes they did. At the time one could take for granted that his own people loved him too, even though he was an autocratic ruler. But that is not so certain any longer; many dispute that belief. Mind you, all this you can see at the museum building nearby; there is an exhibition of photos in his glory! But Koki doesn't like this museum; it is a bit morbid. The whole ground floor is filled with stuffed animals! Poor souls were given to him and died soon after arrival . . . Ah, life is a whore and then you die.

But to all this, Koki says that facts are very boring! They tell you nothing about his character, his habits and passions, his five (or more?) wives. How shrewd he was, how very intelligent, and also how very cruel. How terribly vain and deluded, too. Yes, there are so many more things to know about such a person.

Koki could tell you more about the Marshal because he knew him well. For many years they used to spend hours and hours together over the summer, talking or just contemplating in silence the beauty of the place. And Koki could tell him everything; Koki was a fearless little birdie. After all, why should such a big, historical persona be afraid of Koki's words? Of anybody's words, for that matter? Later Koki understood that being a bird was to his advantage. Had he been a man, his words might have landed him in prison! Yes, that had happened, even with his good friends. You don't agree with him? Off to prison with you! It was that simple.

But though Koki lived in a cage then (and now), and therefore was a kind of prisoner himself, he was free to say whatever he wanted! It is a contradiction to even think about any kind freedom if you are living in a cage, yes. But at least the Marshal would let you think that living in that cage was *your own choice*. Indeed, he spent his life doing just that, making some twenty million Yugoslavs believe they were free. Well, their cage was more colorful than others of their kind, but it was still a cage. Yet people believed him, as did Koki-birdie, too.

After the advent of democracy, every few years another old bugger comes along and takes up residence here. Mercifully, parrots live much longer than men, which means that Koki knows the presidents who have come to the island since the Marshal's time, both of them so far. He knows how different they are from the old one—and how power makes them more similar to him than you would believe. To tell you the truth, by the time Koki adjusts to the new, *elected president* in the Brioni residence (that is the formal difference between the Marshal and these new guys) he is replaced by another. All too soon! It is more comfortable to look at the same face and tell the same jokes for decades, as before, yes? The first to come after the Marshal was his former Communist general-turned-nationalist, an unpleasant, arrogant man with a twisted mouth. Being too lazy to learn new names, this little birdie had high hopes that the man would stay long enough in power for Koki to get used to him. The man himself had even higher hopes! Indeed, Twisted Mouth demonstrated the same intention as the Marshal: to stay in power forever. However, he was far less charming. He suffered from an inferiority complex and went so far as to even order an almost identical uniform as the Marshal's. It was white, like his, with golden epaulettes and lots of medals—he, too, had decorated himself, of course. But in spite of all his efforts, he looked somehow pompous in it. Twisted Mouth was just an imitator, like Koki the parrot, ha ha! Poor man, he almost managed to get elected president for life, but the problem was that his life did not last as long as he surely had expected.

Once, when Twisted Mouth brought some important guests to see him, Koki pretended to be just a stupid parrot and screamed right into his face: "*Long live Comrade Tito! Long live Yugoslavia!*" People here used to shout such slogans on different public occasions. Like during the Marshal's long speeches, a rally organized for his birthday, a May Day parade, or maybe a visit by some foreign dignitary. I could tell that Twisted Mouth hated Koki for that. He seriously lacked a sense of humor. When Koki shouted like that, Twisted Mouth would go pale in the face and point at Koki, his hand shaking with rage. Ooooh . . . Koki would get reeeeeally scared. Koki admits that he's got a loose tongue and tends to make jokes, pretends to be stupid, teases people, even makes them nervous by telling the truth sometimes. That time Koki survived only because he is a popular tourist attraction. One of the exhibits, like the remains of a Roman villa nearby.

Koki did not like Twisted Mouth at all! Maybe because that stuffed bird did not like Koki either? He considered him—Koki!—ridiculous! Perhaps he even considered Koki a traitor? Sometimes Koki thinks these new presidents and their staffs think that just because Koki was the Marshal's trusted companion. How primitive can one get? But everybody who was associated with him is suspect nowadays—even a simple little birdie. On the other hand, Koki tries to understand their paranoia: One has to be watchful! "The enemy never sleeps"—as people used to say during the Marshal's times.

Confidentially, Koki did not like the guys who visited Twisted Mouth either. They were dubious men in black leather jackets speaking to him under their breath, looking around as if they were all part of some great conspiracy. And maybe they were? Then there were other, normal-looking guys in gray suits. Koki could tell that they were foxy old commies who had just switched from the Communist to the new, nationalist ideology. All these guys were somber and grim. Of course, Koki heard why they were of such an unpleasant disposition. These were difficult times for the new president, Twisted Mouth, and his new small state of Croatia—there was a war (or even wars) going on on the mainland, in his formerly beloved Yugoslavia. During his short visits to the Brioni residence Twisted Mouth would get very, very nervous and would talk much, showing maps to the brand-new generals in their brand-new uniforms. Very serious business it was, the war, I mean. During the four war years Koki would not see much of this president and his entourage—or of tourists, for that matter. Twisted Mouth obviously did not care for what this island has to offer, the beauty of nature, of fine food and drink, a nice swim, or a game of golf. I am afraid that with him the former glory of Brioni was gone forever. By the way, did you know that this was home to the biggest golf course in Europe at the beginning of the last century? Yes, very fine people used to come here, aristocrats, millionaires—a great tradition!

Interestingly, Twisted Mouth reminded Koki of the Marshal. Not only because he emulated his looks, but because of his death. Shortly before he ended up in a hospital from which he wouldn't emerge again, he held a press conference. A journalist expressed his concern because the president looked ill, but he rudely replied: "What kind of question is that? Am I not even allowed to have the flu?" However, it was not the flu that killed him but his own disbelief in his mortality. He had an infection but did not take care of it in time. This denial of death is what connects the two of them. The mere idea of it was offensive to both.

. . .

Yes, thinking of glitz and glamour, Koki misses the Marshal. That vigorous, charismatic oldie was interesting and amusing to Koki. But he misses even more the fun of it all—the dinners, guests, strolls, the courting, the gossiping, the beautiful ladies, and the importance this place used to have. However, Koki doesn't say that openly. The current, third president, the Porcupine (Koki's nickname!), is not dangerously suspicious about Koki's "Communist" past. What Koki finds most important about him is that he has a good sense of humor. He would perhaps even understand Koki's reminiscences about "the good old days," though, officially, these were "dark times." According to the new gospel, Yugoslavia was "the prison of the nations," as I heard Twisted Mouth explain to whoever cared to listen. But still, there are people around this quite likable old Porcupine who would promptly brand even a simple little birdie a "Yugo nostalgic"—which is just another word for traitor. Living in a democracy, one would think that a parrot should be entitled to bestow his political and other sympathies freely, to whomever he so pleases—especially concerning the past. But Koki knows better, so he keeps his feelings to himself in order not to—God forbid!—lose his job. He has witnessed that certain things, or should he say, habits, have not changed that much since the Marshal's times. Every new man in power, just like the old one, feels endangered. After all, this state is only a baby state, not even twenty years old. Much younger than Koki himself!

But to whom is Koki telling all this? I see Koki is selling his time too cheaply. Look at you! Do you have a mirror at your hotel?

No, perhaps you don't. Koki knows your kind. You came with a tourist excursion from the mainland and you are staying in a small B&B where they don't have even mirrors. See, Koki has a mirror in his cage and therefore he can see that he is a beautiful white parrot, with a yellow crest, in the middle of his life (he could live more than one hundred years, yes). But you, how do you look with your big stomach, dressed in an old T-shirt and shorts? You look silly. And in those sandals, you look like— well, a catastrophe. Yes. And he'll tell you why. He will if you give him more peanuts, that is! Thanks!

Surely you know that "Brioni" is a sleek fashion brand named after this very island that you are visiting now? It some- how makes sense; Koki knows that the Marshal did not object to fashion. On the contrary, he loved it! He was elegant looking, really debonair. Although he was a Communist, he was a gen- tleman, too. A comrade with style, that is how Koki remembers him—and he is not alone. One of his former friends used to comment that "style and substance eventually became one." Yes, he cared about how he looked; he sometimes changed his suit four times a day. Unlike many of his badly dressed visitors, who would come in gray shiny suits in the middle of the sum- mer. Imagine! When they took off their jackets their shirts would show big sweat stains under their armpits. It revealed their fear. That is, their respect, because in this part of the world fear and respect are one and the same.

Like every autocrat, the Marshal ruled by fear. But could you, please, tell Koki how else one could rule people around here? Tribes need a leader, an authority that has the power to punish them. The big boss in uniform with rows of decorations, that's what they wanted to see. Symbols are important to them. The Marshal knew the mentality of his tribes; he was a pro. His love of fashion was matched only by his love of uniforms. See, he had a great weakness for uniforms. But in his favor, Koki must say that he carried his uniforms with such natural ease and elegance that it amazed people. He also knew that they impressed the populace. On one occasion Koki heard him talking to his biographer, a certain Mister Vladimír. "I remember how much, as a child, I loved looking at the Kaiser," he said. "At that time there were postcards with his picture, in uniform, and he would wear lots of decorations, and we boys in Kumrovec would see them in schoolbooks. Already then I understood that you have to show that you are important, otherwise people won't believe you. You must show that you are above them; otherwise, why should they listen to an ordinary person like themselves? Looks are very important if you want to impress people." And in order to impress them even more, he lived in the former king's palace in Belgrade. A Communist revolutionary living in a palace; that is what I call not only stylish but smart. After all, his people were used to being ruled in monarchic tradition, no? But don't think that the palace or even this residence in Brioni, or any other residence he used, was in his private possession! Oh, no! These official castles and residences (all thirty-two of them) were only at his disposal, that is all. Because it was well known that the Marshal did not need any private property; he lived off of the love of his people, didn't he?

Dressed in his Marshal's gold-ribbed uniform and ordained with many medals—he was one of the largest collectors of medals in history—he emanated authority. The only problem was his belt buckle. It, too, was made of pure gold and, therefore, so heavy that it kept slipping down! That posed a danger to his image—as it would be very unfitting for such a person to lose his pants in public, especially because authority was the main reason for wearing the uniform. But not the only reason! The Marshal was aware that he looked handsome in it: "You know Koki," he used to say, because we often discussed fashion (as well as women!), "when you wear a uniform, you look not only powerful and elegant, but you also feel taller." He was a bit on the short side and sometimes it bothered him a little. He was an accomplished man, but at times he would say such things because he could not do much about his height. "The Marshal walks differently, has a different bearing. Everybody can see that he is an important man," Koki would say. The old man would be pleased with this comment and would give Koki a bite of a tangerine. He himself had grown the fruit and, good person that he was, would donate the whole harvest to orphaned children.

If you ask Koki, the Marshal looked equally elegant in plain clothes, exuding charisma even when wearing shorts. Unlike yours, his shorts were cut to fit—not too tight, not too loose—and made of the finest cotton. Somehow, even his bare legs (in off-white soft leather moccasins, not sandals) did not look as horrible as your bare legs. Or is it that his legs looked good because they belonged to—him? Mmmm, this is something to think about, Koki-birdie!

Koki remembers his stylish white summer suits, tailor-made, of the finest cotton or linen. And his real Panama hat, not like the cheap fake ones I see around nowadays. By the way, speaking of fashion, Koki has noticed that democratization in this particular field means bad quality, don't you think? If democracy in fashion means bad quality and cheap stuff, Koki is not for it. Speaking of democracy, the Marshal was not a democrat, either in fashion or in politics. In both cases, it is better to compare him with real aristocrats in Europe at the time. This all makes one wonder where he got it from—his expensive tastes and political talent. Surely not from his family. He was, as you have already heard, of very humble origin. Koki is not in the mood for deep thoughts, but perhaps his style and talents were innate? Just as some are born with beauty or intelligence, so he was born with good taste and great political talent.

The Marshal was passionate about his looks, women, food, whiskey, and real Havana cigars, straight from Castro. That was the side of him Koki knew best. There were many other sides, too, but Koki-birdie tells what he knows. Maybe he adds a little here and there, but only a little! He doesn't want to appear like a chatterbox or gossip, oh, no!

His sandals? Well, Koki swears to you that the Marshal never wore sandals; he hated them. Maybe because sandals reminded him of his barefoot childhood? Everybody who comes here should know that. You should know it, too. Looking as you do, you would not have made it one thousand meters from here in his time. Soldiers would have shot at you, yes. Not because of the sandals, but because these few islands were off-limits to tourists and proletarians in general. Tell Koki, please, are you wearing sandals so that everyone can see your dirty nails, ha-ha?! No way could you have visited him dressed like that, even if you were president of the universe itself. No sandals, that was an important dress code here.

But it did not apply to the ladies. On the contrary, the Marshal enjoyed a view of their pretty little toes, especially if they were painted red, like those of Elizabeth Taylor. Oh, what a beauty she was! She, with her famous "violet-blue eyes"—Koki heard that expression from the Marshal himself, you know. "I could drown in your violet-blue eyes, my pretty lady!" he told Elizabeth, gallantly kissing her hand the old-fashioned way. She merely laughed in her thin voice. Such a great film star, but her voice was so girlish. "Please, Mister President, call me Liz," she said to him. And then he replied, in his most charming voice: "Only if you call me Joža!" And then Elizabeth tried to pronounce his name in her American way, Y-o-o-u-z-a. Ah, it sounded so sweet. Unlike when Koki would call him . . . All the while they were sitting in his 1953 Cadillac Eldorado. Great car, great! I drove with him a few times around here—it was sensational. He loved that car and polished it himself, whistling a tune, like any ordinary man would, only not many had such a car back then. He then offered to show her the island, and while they drove away into the sunset, I thought, Well, this is just like a Hollywood movie. Maybe this was his thought, too, because he loved the movies, spent a lot of time watching such films, especially westerns.

Thanks for the peanuts; pumpkin seeds are also okay. Listen, today you could hire that very car for five hundred dollars an hour. Isn't that great? Ah, yes, Koki forgets that you don't have that kind of money . . . too bad. This was a unique chance for you to slip into his role!

Yes, it all happened right here, in front of this cage, because he was showing Liz this Koki person. The Marshal was showing off his talking parrot that could swear. But imagine what happened? Koki was so taken by Liz, so confused, that he could not say a word! Much less a bad word in front of such a lady. Perhaps for the first time in his life, Koki was speechless. It took him a while to pull himself together and sing "Jingle Bells," because he could not remember any other song in English at the moment. It was in the middle of the summer when she visited us, and Koki couldn't do better than to sing that stupid Christmas song. How embarrassing! But she was delighted; she kept saying, "Bravo, bravo!"

Liz was so veeery beautiful. Her beauty left many men, let alone this parrot, speechless. It all happened when that husband of hers (was he the fifth? Liz had a tendency to marry many times, just like the Marshal) came here to act in a movie about the German military's attempt to capture the Marshal during World War II. The husband actor, Richard Burton was his name, was playing the role of the Marshal himself, the commander of his partisan army. Koki heard from the Marshal's chambermaid that the Marshal was rather pleased with the film. Later Koki saw the film for himself. Dressed in a well-fitting uniform, Burton really resembled him. Burton was good-looking in a rough kind of way. Pity that he was such a drunkard.

As Koki already told you, he was privileged; he talked freely to the Marshal—as opposed to many of the parrots around him. For example, he would tell him: "Hey, you! Get serious!" Or, "Attention, attention!" That was when his wife was approaching while he was flirting with this or that lady. This often happened when the well-known Italian actress Sophia Loren visited us here. The Marshal loved such fancy company, and she came to Brioni more than once. Whatever the reason for her visit, they enjoyed cooking together. Yes, food, that was another of his favorite pleasures, and if he could combine a beautiful woman with good food—nobody could be happier. The secret with Sophia, besides her long legs, small waist, and big boobs, was that she could cook. They would enjoy preparing food together and his fat wife would kind of supervise them, although she herself did not have the habit of spending time in the kitchen. Later he would eat the pasta that they had cooked together, even if pasta was *not* his favorite food. Neither was fish. Or vegetables, for that matter. Sophia cooked with olive oil. We have excellent olive oil here, produced on the mainland, but it was one of the very few things he could not stand. He was a true son of Zagorje, which is where, on festive days, people eat pig, turkey, chicken, and the like. Oh, he loved to eat roast suckling pig, the ears especially! But chicken, too—grown only for him, it goes without saying. Yet, while cooking with Sofia, he even used to dip his bread into the olive oil and eat it, just to please her. You should have seen his Madame reproaching him for that, telling him, "But you don't like olive oil." "What do you know?!" he would grumble, dismissing her while knowing full well that it was dangerous to do so. Madame could turn his life into hell.

She knew how to make him miserable, and she did it quite

often in his old age. Koki knows that for a fact. Madame was his fifth wife, although I heard that this is disputed. There are stories that he had some seven wives and nineteen children. Koki finds such gossip unconvincing. And by the way, Where are his children now? Did they disappear? His Madame was jealous, that was the problem. Who knows, she might have good reason—and not only regarding film stars. For example, there were two sisters, both his masseuses. They took turns massaging the old man, because he needed a massage twice a day in his old age. These young women did not look bad at all, if you know what Koki-birdie means. Curvy they were, yes! He certainly enjoyed the company of the young ladies. But it was much more important that they had daily access to the Marshal. They had a chance to catch his attention—his ear, as it were. Do you understand? Can you imagine how valuable this was on the favor-exchange market? How many people asked them to speak to him? They could talk to him, tell him this and that, express their opinion about a person or even about politics, why not? They had his attention, which is the only thing that counts. Many courtiers were jealous of this, most of all Madame herself. Koki remembers one particular scene with one of the Marshal's masseuses. Madame raised her voice at these sisters more than once. Koki even heard her screaming once, "Get out, get out you dirty bitch!" She did not choose her words carefully on that particular occasion.

From Lanka, the elephant in our zoo, I heard that once upon a time Madame had been a well-built young beauty who did not know how to swim and had not seen the sea until she came to the Brioni archipelago. At the beginning of their rela-

tionship she was an unassuming peasant girl of exotic beauty—
her thick, shiny black hair was particularly beautiful—who
adored the Marshal. At that young age (she was twenty-three
years old when they met, while he was fifty-five) she was totally dedicated to him. However, Lanka told Koki that with
time she developed into a not very pleasant or charming or
even interesting character, and Lanka should know—she lived
in Brioni longer than Koki. Yet people say that often the Marshal was not nice to his wife either. He could be cynical or
humiliate her publicly, telling her to "just shut up and smile."
She did have a dazzling smile, though.

Koki thinks that it must have been difficult to be his wife.
For one, she wanted children, but he did not. She also must
have become aware of the fact that, without him, she was just a
nobody. With time she probably grew bitter and disappointed
in the deity she had devoted her life to. On the other hand, she
must have been taken in by that glamour and power of his.
With the passing years, as Madame became fatter, her ambitions grew accordingly. Koki developed a theory that her body
mass was somehow related to her desire to rule in his place. But
perhaps Koki is wrong! Anyhow, it was not enough that she
ruled him through his trust in her. She also ruled his office, and
without her approval no one could get a job there. She laid off
people as she pleased; Koki remembers how she chased away
our cook. The woman left in tears, and the Marshal was very
unhappy about the incident. But Madame managed to replace
his security advisers, attachés, and even a longtime secretary, a
very reliable man who did not give her any reason to do that.
Except that he was too close to the Marshal. If he was aware

that she wanted to control the controller the Marshal did nothing to prevent it.

Then, in the seventies, there was a rumor that she had political ambitions. Madame insisted on having a seat in the Central Committee. The only grounds for such a decision was the fact that she was the Marshal's wife. But apparently, as Yugoslavia was not Romania, where Elena Ceausescu even formally shared power with her husband (as a member of the highest party and state institutions), Madame was flatly refused. After that the gossip was that Madame, with a few officers, had even contemplated a coup d'état! If this were true, it would have made Koki wonder if this kind of hunger for power was maybe contagious. But was it true? Koki can only tell you that after 1975 Madame was no longer seen here or in the Marshal's vicinity. Not that Koki was sorry! You see, when Koki met her for the first time, he was just a little birdie, and everybody was nice to him, held him, patted him on his little yellow crest, and played with him. But not her, no sir! She was indifferent to him. Probably in her village in Lika they shot at birds. For Madame, Koki was just that, a bird to shoot at. Oh poor, poor Koki, he could have lost his little head . . . When he inquired among the personnel—Koki always had his trustworthy sources—he heard that she had been removed. Koki swears to you that this was the word they used, *removed* from the palace.

But the conspiracy theory is not likely. Knowing the person, Koki is convinced that in her case the matter was more banal. She was simply jealous of people who managed to get too close to her husband, be they men or women. Sometimes her behavior became farcical: She would brandish her pistol, threatening to kill the masseuse sisters! Even to kill him! "There will be blood!" she allegedly shouted. Now, to threaten to kill a masseuse or two perhaps wouldn't be much of a scandal. But to threaten the Marshal, even if he was her husband—and such fights can happen in a family—that was an entirely different thing. Her threats were taken seriously by his security people, by his doctors, by almost everyone around him. Or perhaps the threats were only used as an excuse to move her away from him—in such cases, one should always consider this possibility.

Ah, you are laughing at this story! Yeah, it sounds kind of funny, the Marshal was already over eighty when the "masseuse incident" happened. However, nothing is funny when it comes to a man in his position. As the result of *putting his life in jeopardy*—this is how it was formulated—Madame was *removed* indeed. Not because she threatened him (or perhaps even plotted to overthrow him); that is legitimate, people do it in every court in the world. But because her behavior was the symptom of a betrayal. Trust is a very precious commodity for a man in power, perhaps the most precious of all. That is why such a man doesn't have friends; he knows that people are motivated by personal interest to befriend him. As a rule, he could never be sure if his best friend wasn't perhaps plotting to take his place. If loyalty is the most appreciated and rewarded quality, then disloyalty is the most severely punished. Even today, after all this time, Koki is convinced that the real problem between them was that the Marshal had trusted Madame and she had let him down. He must have been very sad when he realized that his own wife had betrayed him. That was the main reason she had to go. But he did not send her to a real prison, oh no! Just to a house prison, where she still lives. You did not know that she is still alive? Of course, being so much younger than the Marshal, she has survived him by almost twenty years now. But she never speaks, and when she does, she only complains about how she was treated after his death! You can't hear a word from her about her life with him—or anything else of interest, for that matter. Koki is convinced that she is not allowed to speak; she simply knows too much.

Afterward, people here said that Madame was very lucky. Because, you know, he was not exactly a softie. He could be cruel. He did not hesitate to send a friend to prison for much less. Some of his comrades-in-arms even disappeared without a trace. Not far away from the famous Brioni archipelago, where we are now, was the infamous Bare Island, to name but one such hideous place. It was no more than a piece of stone tossed into the middle of the Adriatic Sea—no trees, no grass, nothing. In 1948, by decree of the Marshal, the most terrible prison one could imagine was established there. Political prisoners were forced to work in a stone quarry and carry heavy stones from one side of the island to the other—and then back again. I know somebody who had a brother, an army officer, who ended up there. By chance, that morning in 1948, he did not listen to the news because he had drunk too much the night before. The price he paid for being uninformed was high: He came to the meeting in his garrison not knowing that during the night the Marshal had split with Stalin. As yesterday's policy had been to align with the Soviets, he expressed his disbelief at the news. Sure enough, he was sentenced as a "Stalinist" and served several years on that wretched island. He was only one of some fifteen thousand who passed through the Bare Island "labor camp," as it was called.

"Our revolution does not eat its children!" the Marshal used to claim at the time. But that simply was not true. The Marshal never appreciated, to put it mildly, opinions different from his. His fear of a so-called counterrevolution was great, although nobody ever defined exactly what that meant. Generally speaking counterrevolution covered just about everything he thought was directed against him, since he personified the Communist Party and the government. Freedom of information was certainly not his kind of thing! Yet in the last ten years of the regime, the party's control mellowed: As long as editors in the media stuck to the general party ideology, they were quite free to publish the news, information, and even critical comments.

The Marshal was a ladies' man, yes he was. He flirted with every woman in sight. Even with such a distinguished person as Britain's Queen Elizabeth. Okay, he didn't exactly flirt, but he did do his best to charm her and many other glamorous and famous ladies. He spoke fluent Russian and German and basic English—not bad for a locksmith. Koki already told you that he was a Communist with style, which made him an exotic bird himself! But in Koki's long life he saw that what attracts people the most is power. Regardless of his looks, charm, or other abilities—of which he apparently had enough—his power itself was magnetic. It pulled people in; it drew them near.

From those exciting times and important visitors to the summer residence at Brioni, Koki remembers the food most of all. It was usually prepared by his cook, a pleasant local woman who understood his fascination, not so much with the food itself, but with its purpose, a feast. A feast meant entertainment, music, meeting interesting people, animated conversations, new faces, new ideas. Such a feast, to be sure, was at the same time a demonstration of his benevolence and his might. An autocrat but a hedonist, a benevolent one compared to Stalin, some say. Koki heard that Stalin's lifestyle was that of an ascetic monk.

You should know that there is a collection of twenty-one thousand menus left from the Marshal! Isn't that an impressive part of his heritage? I could recite to you many of the menus by heart! And the recipes—just ask Koki (and offer him a few nice morsels!). For example, a dinner for Her Majesty Queen Elizabeth consisted of lobster Bellevue, followed by a variation of grilled meat á la Serbe (*čevavapčići, ražnjići, pljeskavice*). On the other hand, Romanian president Nicolai Ceausescu was on a diet, taking only cereal and fruit juice. He was served a simple peasant soup from Zagorje with cheese dumplings. Being of peasant stock, he appreciated it a lot. Indira Gandhi loved apple cake, and Princess Margaret was served quails in their nest.

Ah, Koki could go on listing like this forever . . .

Surprisingly, judging by his favorite foods, the Marshal did not have a very sophisticated palate. He could have had caviar every day. He could have had champagne and strawberries for breakfast every day. What—isn't that the finest breakfast one can have, at least judging by the movies? He could have had anything he wished for. A wag of his little finger would have been enough to bring him quail's eggs, for example, although the thought of eating the poor bird's eggs makes Koki sad. Look, even here, at the seaside—and even in the summertime— his breakfast would typically consist of an omelet with sausages. This was called a *light breakfast*! No wonder his attaché was sometimes desperate, because the doctor's orders were that he should follow a certain diet. But who could have forced the Marshal to diet, even if it was for his own good? Because, of course, only he knew what was best for him, right?

You are what you eat—Koki thinks it must be a Chinese proverb that he heard long ago, because it is so wise. It was certainly true in the Marshal's case. His eating habits were, indeed, very telling for those who knew where to look for signs about his character. As Koki said, pork was his favorite and, as far as he was concerned, his doctors and their ideas about health could rot in hell. His pleasures always came first, and the Marshal certainly knew how to please himself. Koki went so far as to sometimes think that he had become a ruler (a dictator, an autocrat, a head of the state—anyway, a person in power) just to be able to fulfill all his heart's desires. Or was it, again, the same thing as with his legs: Perhaps he acquired such desires only after climbing to power? Never mind, let's not get carried away by such speculation.

It is hard to believe that seemingly unimportant food habits and preferences—the content of his plate—can reveal a person's character. But according to Koki-birdie, his ability to seriously delude himself could have already been detected in his ignoring the doctor's orders and not taking proper care of his health. Knowing that he ate totally inappropriate and harmful food, Koki said to himself, "Our beloved Marshal, the greatest son of our nations and nationalities" (as he was sometimes called) "is seriously infected by the personality cult virus." Ah, I see that you think Koki exaggerates, that he could not be that clever a birdie! But it was easy to come to such a conclusion. The Marshal was an extremely vain man. So much so that he believed nothing bad could ever happen to him. Whatever he did, whatever he ate, no serious illness could befall him. He felt so sure of himself, so untouchable—even by death. And that is the symptom of a grave illness that is closely connected to power. In fact, Koki thinks that it comes from having absolute power. But the paradox of such power is that it clouds not only your judgment but also your image of yourself. You begin to think that "living forever" is not only a metaphor; you begin to live that metaphor!

The most important characteristic of the personality cult is that a person believes in his own immortality. After he died, one of his doctors was here, and Koki heard him say that the Marshal did not believe he was dying. "What, amputate my leg? I'd rather kill myself!" he said angrily when the doctors told him he would need an operation to save his life. What kind of life would that be? Koki knows that the Marshal loved traveling, and he could see how humiliating it would be for him to travel like an invalid! A crippled old man! And how could he lead his people, who were accustomed to a strong, decisive, imposing person? It would look disgraceful. So it took quite some persuasion to get him to agree to surgery. He wanted to be the only one in charge of his destiny, like God. And even when he survived that first surgery, the Marshal was not aware of death looming— he spoke about his future plans, Koki heard. For him, death was an abstraction; it concerned others—not him. Yes, he said that "one is immortal because of one's deeds," but this did not apply to him. Mind you, on his deathbed his barber dyed his hair every second week! That is what Koki calls wishful thinking. A sad picture comes to Koki's mind from those times, a photo with his two sons from the hospital in Ljubljana. The Marshal's last photo. Koki could see on their faces that they were worried and sad, that they knew what he did not want to comprehend, that this was the end.

Koki also thinks that at the beginning others were to blame for adoring the leader. But later on, he himself became responsible for accepting that adoration, for believing in it. One of the dangers of the Marshal's attitude toward the future was reflected in his perception of himself as being irreplaceable. That perhaps determined the destiny of his beloved country, Yugoslavia: He was hardly capable of imagining its future without him. Therefore, he did not prepare his successor. To create a successor would have meant that he recognized the fact that he was on his way out. But wouldn't that mean defeat? Perhaps even an offense? He could not stand competition; therefore, he eliminated anyone who had the capacity of eventually replacing him. Another characteristic of his personality cult was that he could not be criticized—a luxury others didn't have.

Then, in the late seventies, a so-called collective presidency of eight men, who would rotate in ruling the country, was created. But this eight-headed monster survived only a short time before the country collapsed into its bloody wars.

.   .   .

Well, well, of course Koki knows that in telling you all this he is being indiscreet. But, after all, the Marshal is dead, and this way he gets some extra food. He is a pragmatic tourist worker, and this is the only reason he is talking to you (by the way, give him a piece of your apple; he loves apples!). Koki, the Marshal's parrot who speaks five languages, and is a conversationalist and entertainer of movie stars and statesmen, of queens and dictators, reduced to the role of a clown for a fistful of peanuts now. Sad, very sad . . . no wonder Koki gets depressed sometimes. But then, there is YouTube, his favorite Web site. Koki asks an old zookeeper to bring him to a computer at the reception desk of the hotel. The keeper knows that when Koki gets sentimental, he asks a young receptionist to show him films of the Marshal's speeches and interviews. Or—if Koki is really in a gloomy mood—even of his funeral. Strange, you might think, that a depressed birdie would watch the funeral, yes? But let Koki tell you, it actually lifts our spirits, the zookeeper's and Koki's. This is because they can remind themselves how much the Marshal was loved and respected. Regardless of current claims to the contrary, every single man and woman cried when the Marshal died. Imagine that moment, when more than twenty million people cried! It was splendid, just splendid to see. Koki remembers how on May 4, 1980, life stopped in the whole country, which was much bigger then. And how people behaved as if they had lost their father, which in a way was true.

Yes, Koki knows that you are about to ask him why they cried for the old dictator, with his royal splendor and his personality cult? For good reason, though: He gave them a good life. Most of the people in Yugoslavia were peasants who had moved to cities after World War II but remembered their hard lives in the villages. The Marshal spoiled them. Like him, they enjoyed life far beyond their means. That is why the political opposition never blossomed in this country. People were satisfied with their lives, with their standard of living. They were happy to travel abroad. To wear blue jeans and Italian shoes. To read foreign books and newspapers, watch movies and TV programs from the West. With these crumbs of freedom Yugoslavia differed from the Soviet bloc countries. How little a difference it was—and how big at the same time!

Yet, this moment of his death and the paralysis of the whole of Yugoslavia was perhaps the finest moment, the height of his personality cult. Just as if the Marshal belonged to some great royal family, say the Romanoffs or the Habsburgs. If only the Marshal could see it, Koki is sure he would be really pleased with himself. Over 200 foreign delegations attended his funeral, as well as 127 heads of state. Whether you believe it or not, that was more than at Churchill's or Kennedy's funerals. Maybe because he was the symbol of a "third way" at a time of polarization for many poor nations, regardless of the fact that this way led nowhere in the end. Anyway, the whole world was in Belgrade that day, as we used to say here at his residence at Brioni. Yes, his funeral was quite a spectacle, and it made Koki proud. Even more so because Koki knew some of the attending dignitaries personally. In a way, if one could forget the sadness of the occasion, it was a magnificent event. Surely never to be repeated for any of the buggers whom Koki would later see on this island in his long life.

No doubt, the citizens of the many small states that emerged from the breakup of Yugoslavia will judge the Marshal's role in history and the controversies surrounding his rule. These days, Koki hears that they are asking themselves whether he was a great Communist leader or a crook—as if the two were mutually exclusive! In the end, let me tell you that Koki doesn't want to get involved in such matters. Koki the parrot, his court jester, knows only that he did not need to beg for food back then. He performed for food, yes, but he did not beg.

No, thanks, I've had enough of your peanuts for today. Now, fuck off and go wash your feet!

III

THE BEAR AND THE PRINCESS OF LIGHT

My name is Tosho, Tosho the Dancing Bear. My stage name, that is; otherwise I am Todor. As in Todor Zhivkov, our beloved Bay Tosho, our Tato. I was named after him by a toothless old Gypsy Roma fittingly named Angel. Angel belonged to the only nonintegrated people in Europe, the one that managed to resist the Communists' attempts at social engineering to create "new men"—as well as any other kind of social integration. He bought me from hunters and brought me up and trained me to dance. His family had owned bears for seven generations; we were their only source of income. Angel loved Todor Zhivkov, the first secretary of the Communist Party, the president of Bulgaria, and the most reliable ally of the USSR in the Soviet bloc. He is one of those who claims that during the thirty-three years of Zhivkov's rule he felt more of a human being than he does today. By that he means that all of his eleven children went to school, even if only for a year or two. Health care, housing, employment opportunities, and social welfare—all of it was more available to his people before. Nowadays, however, said

Angel, in the new, united Europe we are being persecuted more and more. Not only in Bulgaria, but all over Eastern Europe. In Hungary and Slovakia, in the Czech Republic, Romania, and Slovenia we are being expelled, beaten, stabbed, forcibly sterilized, shot dead, or burned alive in arson attacks. Our kids are still placed in schools for the handicapped, which predetermines their future . . . But maybe his memory is failing him. Anyway, twenty years after Zhivkov has been gone from power, he still keeps a newspaper clipping of Bay (Uncle) Tosho's photo taped on the wall, right above his black-and-white TV set.

Now I live near Beltisa, in a beautiful park and resort—a destiny I share with some twenty other colleagues in the dancing profession. It is our new home, created especially for us—with the help of some European foundation, I assume. But as I get easily bored in this paradise, I decided to write a book of testimonies about life in captivity before the fall of Communism. Inevitably, that means writing about people as well. How could I avoid them? They held us captive, but our destinies were intertwined in so many other ways, too. It is not easy to understand that they also suffered. Because, even though they were the subjugators of animals, they were captives as well.

As my front paws are good for nothing because of my rheumatism, I am forced to dictate this manuscript to a pleasant young girl, an animal rights activist who comes here to help feed us. Evelina brings me apples and grapes, my favorite fruits. She is twenty years old—still almost a cub in human terms. At the beginning of this project it moved me to see how distressed she was by my stories, how hard it was for her to learn that we had suffered so much. But then I realized that she was troubled not only by the fact that we had been tortured, but also that we had withstood torture without even a squeak. She could not understand our passiveness. Evelina belongs to a new generation that grew up after the fall of Zhivkov's regime, free from Communist Party ideology. I realized that recently, when she asked me, "But why didn't you do something? You are so much bigger, so much stronger than the people who held you imprisoned!" Yes, why didn't we? "I'll tell you why, young lady: Because the thought never occurred to us, that's why! That was the secret of both Zhivkov's and Angel's rule—not only was your body captured, but so was your mind. I learned only in hindsight that what keeps one enslaved is one's own captive mind," I told her. "And if you are still wondering, Was there no one else to stand up for our rights, no one to stop this unbearable torture?—like neighbors or the police, or other citizens— I tell you: No! They all watched us dance and laughed! It amused them to see a huge and dangerous animal reduced to a pitiful clown. It proved their domination. A sad story of how beastly people can be, given the chance."

Ah, it is perhaps useless to try to tell new kids what it was like to live before, to dance while somebody else yanks your chain . . . Nevertheless, I see it as my task. "You need to know that, you need to remember," I say to Evelina, and she smiles at me with her beautiful, innocent smile, that of a child who doesn't know what I am talking about. But all the while she understands the suffering of defenseless animals better than the suffering of the people. I must say that she has a point there. From where she stands, it is not easy to see that Bulgar-ian people were treated pretty much like us. They could not do much to change *their* own condition as "dancing bears," so to speak. And maybe, after all, they did not want to.

My life with Angel, his big family, and his five dogs, of which Dobri was my best friend was . . . how can I put it? Once I was tamed, I guess it was bearable. Yes, the word is bearable. It means that I got used to such a life, one gets used to any-thing. We traveled a lot; he played the *godoulka* fiddle and the drum while I danced. On a good day Angel would collect de-cent money and then he would be nice to me. In the evening we would eat together and get drunk on beer, and sometimes even on his favorite brandy, *rakija*. On a bad day he would curse my laziness and my bitch of a mother. That would make me sad. But at least he did not beat me. I knew that it was cus-tomary to beat us dancers, and I must admit that I was grateful to Angel that he did not practice it.

I was the most famous dancing bear in the whole of Bul-garia. We traveled from his village in the mountains to the sea-side, to Varna, Plovdiv, Blagoevgrad, Ruse, even to Sofia. I remember how curious and excited I was when I was young, and I must say that I learned to enjoy such a life sometimes. In the years after the collapse of the Zhivkov regime, we were even filmed several times by foreign TV crews. Angel naively believed this would contribute to my fame and his budget— and even to Bulgarian tourism. But it proved to be exactly the opposite, because this led animal rights activists straight to us later on . . .

I believed that Angel and I were friends after all those years of living and performing together. This in spite of the fact that he kept me on a chain, with a ring through my nose. He convinced me that it was more for the sake of appearance. "This is for your own safety, eh! People would go mad if they saw a bear walking free in the street," he used to say, reassuringly. "They would kill you right away. People are cruel, believe you me. I have seen it many times in my life." As if I did not know that!

I met with human cruelty for the first time when my mother was killed. It was a beautiful spring day, and we had just climbed up to a hill when we heard a strange sound. Only one shot was fired, and our mother collapsed right in front of us. I still remember her last glance at us, full of despair. My sister and I spent a day hiding in a cave nearby. We were small cubs, alone, hungry, and frightened. The hunter's dogs found us. I never saw my sister again, and for a while I kept wondering if perhaps she had become a dancer, too? Or was she living in a cage in a zoo or, even worse, in a circus? I asked my young friend Evelina, did she know what a circus was. To my surprise she answered that she had only seen it on TV. Of course, she added, she would never, ever go to see poor tamed animals performing ridiculous and humiliating tasks. True, I agree that these animals are much worse off. I sometimes think of lions and elephants freezing during our long winters, and I don't know how they can survive. Perhaps I should collect their testimonies, too? Although here, in this refuge, I have heard enough terrible stories from other bears, as each of us has our own to tell.

Angel kept me in the yard together with his five dogs. In the beginning I thought I was a dog! And day after day, he also taught me how to dance. He said that he needed to teach me to dance in order to go around and make money with me. I must say that I don't like to go back to that particular memory of my torture, of jumping like crazy on a hot metal plate while listening endlessly to his fiddle . . . This is how they trained us: They either heated a large piece of metal or just spread hot coal on the ground, and then forced us to step on it and "dance." We bears immediately realized that it was better to spare at least two paws, so we would stand up on our hind legs and lift first one, then the other. It looks like dancing to people, I guess. For some reason it even makes them laugh. All I can say is that it is unbearably painful. Afterward you lie in a corner, half dead, licking your blisters and the raw flesh of your wounds . . . and you are only a baby. But it was useless to expect pity; in a traditional peasant society there is no pity for either domestic or wild animals. They are there to be used and abused. They must be made useful. In their Marxist lingo, it was called "productive labor," I remember. Even a dog, the first domesticated animal ever, has to work. He guards the house or the herd. A cat catches mice. No place for pets in the countryside! A child plays with a chicken and has it for soup the next day. Most animals are bred to be killed, anyway. The only difference is that domestic animals are rarely tortured the way we were.

But in the beginning of the seventies a change happened in Bulgaria, when Lyudmila Zhivkova, the daughter of Todor Zhivkov, was appointed to a number of high party and state offices. She was installed in high positions while her relatives occupied lower ones. Her appointment was not at all unusual; when a king or a dictator does something like that, it is hardly a surprise. After all, Bulgaria was not alone in this; such was the custom in other, similar societies, like Romania and Albania. But the difference was that Lyudmila was not incompetent. On the contrary, she was a historian by training, and even wrote a few books (supposedly with a little help from her staff). She studied history in Sofia and Moscow, and even spent some time at Oxford University researching a book about Turkish-Bulgarian relations. From 1972 on, and within a very short period of time, Lyudmila became: chairwoman of the Committee for Culture; a member of the Central Committee and the Politburo; chairwoman of the Commission for Science, Culture, and Education; the People's representative (MP) in their Parliament; and a member of the Council of Ministers. In 1975 Lyudmila became the minister of culture.

I know that many saw her for what she really was: a second generation of the Communist *nomenklatura* children, groomed to become the heir to her father's throne. At that time Bulgarians did not live in the twentieth century, as people call it— we bears count time differently. They were stuck in medieval times, when the country was treated as the private property of a family, and power was handed down from father to son. Or, in the case of Lyudmila, to daughter. In many old Bulgarian folk songs, a woman is a magical creature, a mediator between the earth and the sky, between the natural and the supernatural. Such a woman is called a *samodiva*, or a wild fairy, and she possesses the untamed spirit necessary to maintain balance in the universe. It turned out that Lyudmila did indeed act as if she were a *samodiva*, linking two totally opposite worlds, one material and the other mystical and occult. Raised with the atheism and materialism of Marxist dogma, she embraced the opposite: yoga, Hinduism, and Buddhism, as well as the folk medicine of Peter Dinev and the prophecies of Vanga, an allegedly clairvoyant illiterate peasant woman.

In fact, the story of Lyudmila reminds me of our old fairy tales . . . In my view, a fairy tale about her would run somewhere along the following lines:

Once upon a time, in the faraway land of the dictatorship of the proletariat, beneath the Balkan mountain there lived a young woman by the name of Lyudmila. She was not a beauty, but she was quick, intelligent, and ambitious. Moreover, she was a princess, the apple of the eye of the mighty King Todor I. After finishing her education and becoming learned in history and many other important, not to mention unimportant, subjects, one day she approached her father with a plan. "Beloved father," she said, "I have thought long and hard about how to improve the lot of our people." Her words caught the king's attention, and he was delighted, as he himself had devoted his whole life to this very aim, alas not very successfully. His kingdom was a sad place, where people and animals dwelled in misery. Something needed to be done before his subjects, having nothing to lose, would rise up and start to rebel against him. Something that would make them love their king even more. "I know how to turn them into harmonious human beings, full of celestial light and eternal beauty. The whole universe would rejoice in our new life of wisdom, truth, and spirituality!" the princess explained to her father.

These words sounded strange to the king's ears, which were used to a very different vocabulary, but what the heck? If his little darling could do something to change life in the kingdom—even if only in spirit—so much the better. He knew that in order to accomplish this she had to become the high commander of culture. The Council of Elders, or Politburo, approved his decision instantly. Of course, it was merely a formality. So the princess, the apple of the king's eye, presented to the council her master plan of improving the soul of the entire nation. "Balance will reign in our beloved Bulgaria," she promised them. The old men applauded; they could do nothing else anyway. They were experienced enough to know that the new language she spoke, and which they could not understand—and were sure that nobody else could either—carried an important message: In real life nothing much would change for them. Or for other subjects, for that matter.

Princess Lyudmila threw herself into her work. She dispatched envoys to bring to her the best scientists and artists, the most distinguished writers and academics, and the finest intellectuals. They together would create magnificent plans and programs to implement beauty in the everyday life of the people—especially through education. For it was clear to her that one has to start with young minds not yet molded by reality . . .

Some of these envoys she sent abroad to search for

beauty and light there, as she herself did by traveling to exotic kingdoms like India and Nepal, many days ride by horseback. More important still, she reached out to the people. In her speeches she tirelessly and enthusiastically explained how they could benefit from the creative powers of spiritual change that each of them possessed within themselves—it only needed to be awakened. Everywhere the princess went she was met by enthralled masses of people; it was a sign that she was speaking straight to their souls. It was so evident to her that her subjects and her country needed a spiritual renaissance, and she often wondered how it was that nobody had understood this before her.

Among all these frantic activities she found time to marry, divorce, remarry, and have two children. However, she expressed the desire for her private life to be kept out of the public arena. . . .

The ambitious princess, the apple of the king's eye, was capable of rising even higher above the harshness of reality. She wanted to present the little kingdom of Bulgaria to the world, as this was the home of great Thracian treasures, and of beautiful orthodox icons. Under her supervision and command, exhibitions sprang up and traveled around the world. The king had to squeeze money from his subjects, but that was never a problem when a higher cause demanded of them such a sacrifice. The most important of her many projects was the celebration of the thirteen hundredth anniversary of Bulgarian statehood. But the neighboring Great Soviet Empire was not really pleased with Lyudmila's barely concealed nationalist projects. They thought that the planned celebration was a daring display of Bulgarian national identity. As if Bulgaria were an independent kingdom and not merely one of its many satellites! Such an act was dangerous, because it could inspire other Eastern European satellites to think that they, too, could have an identity (and life!) separate from the Great Soviet Empire. That simply could not be allowed. Especially because there were signs that the princess might be the next in line for the throne and—according to spy reports of the time—she was but a dangerous lunatic.

A cunning plan was put into action. Lyudmila's lover, Alex, was one of the Soviets' many men in Sofia. They wanted to install him in power after the king's death. They instructed Alex to talk Lyudmila into an attempt to overthrow King Todor I, whereupon he would take over power. But her pride was hurt: She had envisioned this position for herself! When the plan was discovered (perhaps thanks to her hurt pride?), the king went mad with fury. Yet he forgave his daughter, as he knew that her heart was full of love for him, for his kingdom, the whole world, and even the universe. "My dear child, all in good time! The throne will not escape you. You have proven to me that you are worthy of it," he told his daughter. Lyudmila was relieved. Being the harmonious creature that she was, she did some more yoga stretches and meditated a bit upon the divine and eternal—and for her, the matter was settled.

But not for Alex, who understood that his Politburo career, if not his life, was at stake. What was to be done? He contacted his patrons, and they came up with yet another devious plan. Of course, in such medieval states, the custom was simply to resolve such complications with murder. But they did not put it so bluntly to Alex. In the meantime, who knows, he might have been influenced by all this light and beauty blah-blah of the princess. The Soviet secret police, the KGB, gave him a small crystal vial in a red velvet box. Allegedly, Alex was told that it was a magic potion. Once Lyudmila opened and smelled it, she would fall in love again and help him to the throne.

When Lyudmila, busy with preparations for the anniversary exhibition, received his gift, she was very pleased. She took it as a sign of remorse. Being a woman, she could not resist but to open the bottle right away, believing that it was a perfume. The sweet fragrance enveloped her. *He still loves me*, she thought, before her spirit left her body, only to become one with the universe—as she herself would have put it. She was thirty-nine years old . . . When the servants entered her chamber, her body was gone. No one noticed the small green frog that jumped through the window into the garden.

After her disappearance, darkness fell upon the kingdom. It lasted for the next eight years, when a new light descended upon Bulgaria, this time from the West.

"I think that we Bulgarians were blessed with her in a strange way. She had the power to do more bad things than she did. That is why I like the idea that she did not die of poison (which is only one of the many versions of her death), but rather turned into a small, fragile green frog—into a little animal, that is," I told Evelina. "Ah, yes, how very typical of Bulgaria! Unlike in other fairy tales, in this one the princess turns into a frog and not the other way around. I like your interpretation!" exclaimed Evelina, not really knowing much about the said Princess Lyudmila.

But she really did behave more like a princess than a party bureaucrat. Regardless of whether she was allowed (or not) to behave differently because she was protected by her omnipotent father, the truth is that she was educated, intelligent, and ambitious. Bringing a whiff of modernity to Bulgarian art and culture was a very positive attempt.

Even if her ideas were often very, very strange.

Take her "national program for aesthetic education," as part of the "construction of a mature socialist society." As much as she tried to put it into practice, her directions were vague and abstract. No wonder, because it was not an easy task to link "development according to the law of the spiral" with development according to the dominating laws of economic determination in Marxism: The material world represents the "base," while the "fluffy" stuff of culture, beauty, and spirit belongs to the "superstructure."

Or take her rhetoric. Her rhetoric was delightfully fuzzy and deceptive. Here is a quote from a 1980 analysis by the journalist Jordan Kerov, which Evelina found somewhere for me (I think she called the place the "Internet," but I don't know where it is situated):

> Lyudmila Zhivkova's opening speech at the 1979 "Banner of Peace Assembly" in Sofia, for example, contained the following words or concepts taken directly from the oriental mystics or from their occidental proponents: harmony, harmonious development of man, and perfection, etc. (occur 33 times); light, celestial light, brightness, etc. (35 times); the Universe, the Planet, the Galaxy, Endlessness, the Infinite, the Eternal, Nature etc. (33 times); Beauty, Truth, etc. (38 times); Wisdom (19 times); creative powers, dreams, aspirations, etc. (36 times); and Spirit, vibrations, energy, blessing, etc. (16 times).
>
> Lyudmila Zhivkova also uses phrases like the "effulgent purposefulness," the "sonorous vibration of the seven-stage harmony of the Eternal," and the "vibrations of the electrons." All this she managed to put together in a speech lasting only about 15 minutes and, which is the most amazing, addressed to children of up to 14 years of age.

Even if I try very hard, I just can't imagine Madame Ceausescu or Madame Hoxha giving a similar speech in front of children or workers or Communist Party members or the Politburo. Many compared her to the powerful wives of other leaders, like Nexhmije, the wife of the first secretary of Albania, Enver

Hoxha. Or like the notorious Elena Ceausescu. Both of them had power but didn't even attempt to do anything good with it. Unlike women in positions of power acquired through their relationships with dictators, Lyudmila did something good, at least in one particular field. In spite of her folly, her reign as the minister of culture is nevertheless considered the golden age of art and culture in Bulgaria. Artists traveled abroad to study, and abstract art was exhibited in galleries—unheard-of in the other satellite states. Under her reign, a national palace of culture was constructed and the National Gallery of Art was replenished with formidable works of art. The exhibition "Thracian Gold Treasures from Bulgaria" traveled to twenty-five cities around the world, and many countries also saw the fine exhibition of Orthodox icons. Last but not least, a big "manifestation," "Banner of Peace, World Children's Assembly," was held in Sofia, under the auspices of the United Nations Educational, Scientific and Cultural Organization (UNESCO).

At a time of such a feudal type of rule as Zhivkov's in Bulgaria, of strong oral tradition, myths, folk songs, and fairy tales— because in spite of all the lip service, none of this was eradicated by the decades of socialist government—it was also normal to keep dancing bears.

Why, then, did we animals see in Lyudmila the possibility of salvation at all? I think we believed that, if she understood art and beauty and their importance in life, there was hope for this society and its primitive treatment of animals. Not to mention the fact that her father, like all other Communist heads of state, was a hunter! But she believed that animals have souls! Surely she would do something about bears dancing under her nose with burned paws and bleeding noses? If only she knew about us! If only the ruler knew the real condition of his subjects, he would change it, for sure. Rulers are just. Surely she was just. Or so we hoped for a while.

I must say that, frankly, I was impressed that she was a vegetarian. This custom was pretty much unheard-of in Bulgaria. Yes, there were some sensitive souls who couldn't eat meat because it belonged to a slaughtered animal. Instead of a piece of meat on the plate, they would see a little calf calling for its mother. But such individuals were few and far between. People ate meat if they could buy it; anything else was considered to be eccentric and likely to be ridiculed, maybe even declared as the "decadent influence of the capitalist West."

At first I thought that to be a vegetarian in a country where many people could not afford to eat meat—where such a diet was not a matter of taste or choice—was an extraordinary, enlightened decision. You have to be really high-minded and spiritually oriented. Because vegetarianism is more than a diet—for example, as when an ill person is prescribed vegetarian food. It is also more than a taste preference, like when you do not enjoy the taste of meat. It is an ideology, and it fit well with her other ideologies. But apparently I was wrong. Long after Lyudmila was gone I understood how easy it had been for her to be a vegetarian. She defended the rights of other living beings, mostly mammals, because animals are like people; they feel pain, they feel fear. Therefore, she appeared more human herself. On the other hand, she did nothing to change their conditions. Her activity in our favor was restricted to just that—not eating meat. And hoping that one day everybody would come to the conclusion that it is not moral to feed on creatures that endure as much pain as humans do.

I naively imagined how, for example, she could have given the order to ban the capture and torture of wild bears. Or, for that matter, to let people travel abroad and then decide for themselves what beauty and light and harmony are. But this would have required much more from her than grand words. It would have also been more dangerous to deal with human than with animal rights. At the time, human life was seldom perceived in its single form; it was usually seen as only a mass, a crowd. Our princess fled to the safe sphere of the spirit and light. When she spoke, it was in the lofty language of symbols and poetic metaphors. There was no real change; there could not be any. In the end, even if her intentions were good, our life went on without change. Freedom—be it for animals or for humans—was not her priority. How could it be? She had little or no contact with real life, with real underdogs and underbears. She simply *did not see us as being enslaved*. The simple truth was that socialist leaders could not care for us animals because they did not care for people either. We were all the same to them.

As far as my life was concerned, darkness fell upon it, too. And so it remained until a year ago, when activists from the Free Bears Now! organization come to rescue me from Angel. They saw that fatal TV footage of me dancing in Sofia and tracked us down. Apparently, I was one of the last dancing bears in the

Balkans to be saved. Now I see that it was about time for my rescue, because I am old, exhausted, and in pain.

Anyway, at first I did not want to leave Angel for a better (but unknown) life in a resort. So when two activists visited us, both Angel and I tried to reason with them. Angel swore on his life that I am to him like his own child, that he feeds me the very food he eats. Of course, he was exaggerating. He fed me mostly stale bread and leftovers from their disgusting, unhealthy, sometimes carnivorous meals. He even shed a tear or two for me. Angel could shed tears whenever; I never understood this ability of people and how tears could be taken seriously as an argument among their kind. I, on the other hand, tried to verify his story in a way these young people might perhaps understand, so I displayed my figure and fur and bared my poor teeth as proof. But the iron ring in my nose, and the fact that Angel kept me chained to a mulberry tree in front of his shack, spoke strongly against him. In the end, the older of the two, a serious, businesslike young man, gave Angel an offer he could not refuse: a lump sum of money as compensation. He actually was not in a position to argue, because dancing bears had become outlawed, anyway. Plus, Angel badly needed to repair his roof. Even though Gypsy Roma people are famous for their disregard of the law, my transfer was duly arranged. I was not asked for an opinion, of course. Democracy yes, but not for bears!

Ah, the wheel of fortune—or, perhaps, the wheel of history?—turns in unpredictable ways.

Before they left, and while Angel was signing the papers for my release, the young activist said, "We especially care about these poor beasts because they symbolize the Bulgarian people, whom Todor Zhivkov kept chained!" Well, he couldn't resist an ideological statement, could he? I guess he meant that people under Zhivkov did what he wanted and never rebelled against him. True, very true! The other side of this picture was, however, reflected in Angel's case, where the socialist government provided the basic (bare) necessities for them. Most people, not only this Gypsy Roma, valued that. I know it from my own experience: however meager the provisions you get, if you get them regularly, they make you feel safe. Before, it was a simple trade-off: One traded one's freedom for security. After all, what is freedom without anything to eat? I must add that my friend Evelina strongly disagreed with me. She repeatedly shook her head, exclaiming that never, ever would she trade freedom for anything. But saying "never" in such an adamant way is so typical of young people, simply because they have no idea what they are talking about.

Was I truly rescued as a symbol of a society? Then and there, I understood that it is hard for past and present to meet. The bear-rescuing mission was some kind of a new dogma for these youngsters. While people are left to struggle for survival in the jungle of the market economy, it is the turn of the animals to be taken care of and sheltered. A new, free generation just assumes that in a democracy people should take care of themselves.

Seriously speaking, it was not easy to leave the old man, his people, and his village. "You obviously repressed the fact that he was actually your torturer. You developed a *Pavlovian reflex*," said Evelina. She learned about that at school, I guess.

"This is why even today you start dancing whenever you hear the *godoulka* or any other kind of music playing." She was talking about a recent event when she had brought her iPod and let me listen to some rock music. I started to dance with the iPod in my paw and the headset on. It was grotesque, I know, but the urge to dance was stronger than my will to resist it. She was saddened by this episode, and so was I. Indeed, I think that she might be right. A hot-metal training plate had been installed in my brain forever. This might be the reason why I don't think that I can fully understand and appreciate the new freedom I enjoy. Besides, every freedom has its limits. But I am an old bear; there is no salvation for old bears trained to dance even when no one is yanking their chain.

As if that diagnosis were not enough, Evelina concluded that I had probably developed the "Stockholm syndrome" as well. This is when a victim identifies with his captor, and even feels grateful to him. The young man from Free Bears Now! was definitely right. In that respect, I surely represent the Bulgarian people from the time of socialism. Except, perhaps, for the Gypsy Roma people, who never really fit into that system. They were indifferent to the government ideology, they just got used it—and I respect them for that. By the way, I noticed that Angel and his family have not been saved by anyone so far. There are not many—in any case, not enough—special organizations I know of that protect the rights of Gypsies Roma, even if they are the most discriminated against minority in Europe today. Unlike us, they are humans, and they are supposed to integrate into the society. But as Angel once said to me, "What if I don't want to integrate? What if we want to go on and live the way our people have lived for thousands of years? Who is going to protect our right to live as we want?" Today, when I know more about the outside world, I could tell him: not many. You have to protect your rights yourself, because you Gypsy Roma, it seems to me, are a kind of modern-day wild bear. And the hunt is on.

IV

THE CAT-KEEPER IN WARSAW

(Letter to the State Prosecutor)

Sir,

I am addressing your office and you personally in connection with case No. PT/2875/2008-09, regarding the defendant whom I, for reasons of my own, will address only as the General here. As you are well aware, in the autumn of 2008 the Institute of National Remembrance, investigating Nazi- and Communist-era crimes, brought in an indictment against a total of nine persons. Now the eighty-six-year-old General, who headed the Military National Salvation Council, created on December 13, 1981, stands accused, among other things, of leading this "criminal organization"—for which he could get up to ten years in prison.

I will abstain from any comment about this institute and its methods in conducting the *lustration* process— perhaps it is enough to mention that I have heard some humans call it the "Ministry of Truth." But, on the other hand, I do not go out in the streets of Warsaw very often, and it could be that I am missing some valuable information.

I am appealing to you because I believe it is extremely important to bring the case of the General urgently to an end. I will try to explain why.

Sir, you rightly might ask who am I to take it upon myself to address you at all? Therefore, please allow me first to introduce myself. My name is Gorby. I am a female of feline origin—what you humans call cats. Being born in the house of the General's daughter, I have been living in the General's household for almost ten years now. His whole family loves animals; the General himself, unfortunately, favors horses the most. No wonder. He is an officer, after all. Let me explain our relationship: I am considered to be the General's pussycat, although I take a somewhat different view of this myself. From my standpoint I was nice enough to choose to live in his home, and to allow him and everybody else to believe just the opposite. It is perhaps too banal to say that I picked him up, since it is well known that we cats are free spirits, unlike dogs, of course. But I have to share the house with his dog, Napoleon. This is because Napoleon Bonaparte is the person the General admires the most. Not a good choice of a name, because Napoleon is a big, dumb mongrel. The only certain thing about his lineage is that he evidently belongs to the shallow end of a gene pool. Of course, his favorite activity is playing with a ball! The poor thing shows no sign of intellectual activity whatsoever, and I can tell that he bores the General. Who wouldn't be bored by throwing about that round object again and again? But I have some use for him; he brings me news and information from the outside world—as my courier, you might say.

I, on the other hand, am never either bored or boring. You are arrogant, I've heard Napoleon say about me more than once behind my back, but it is not my intention here to gossip about him. I just want to stress the fact that it was my *choice* to live with the General. *To choose* is a very important verb for me. I have no problem with freedom, since I did not live in that allegedly *inhuman* period of human history called Communism. I have often heard this adjective—by "inhuman" humans mean "animal-like." Let me take a chance here to express my total disagreement with this use of the word; it should be corrected! Needless to say, we animals rarely exercise your bloody habit of killing each other within the same species. With the exception of fighting dogs, but those gladiators are beyond contempt, I am afraid.

Going back to my relationship with the General, I cannot say that he is my butler, although it is very close to the truth; it would offend him if I were to claim that. The General is very much a person of the old times. By that I mean that he is truly sensitive to class differences, maybe even more so because he was born into a noble family. *Noblesse oblige!* So, let's just simplify things and state here that the General is my keeper.

With this introduction, I would like to move to the purpose of my letter and offer you some of my feline reflections.

Let me tell you, Sir, that I have two reasons for submitting this appeal to you. The first one is strictly personal. Right now, the General is in the hospital with a severe case of pneumonia and various other ailments that I don't want to bother you with. This is not the first time; his age and the stress of this trial are wearing him out. Pneumonia can cause the death of an old and frail person. Considering his poor health throughout his whole life, I am seriously worried that he might not ever make it to hear the sentence when it is given out. Especially because I know that in this country such trials can drag on for years. Indeed quite some time elapsed from the first indictment to the beginning of his trial . . . I would hereby like, as his friend—indeed his *confidant*—to submit this appeal for you to take matters into your own hands and bring a quick decision in whatever direction you see fit.

My second reason is of a more general nature, though. I see the young generation of Poles: for them Communism is something that died twenty years ago, before they were even born. It is passé! But although this young generation might not be very knowledgeable or even interested in the events of the past, they should be responsible for how they deal with their past *now*. Therefore, the trial of the General is a very important example for them.

Speaking of the General, I ask myself if he (and others from his time) should have been put on trial at all—and what is such a trial expected to achieve? To make my point clear, I do think that a fair trial makes it possible for an unjustly accused person to exonerate himself. Yet, I wonder if the General should have been put on trial in a criminal court. Let's make no mistake here—the General welcomes his trial. "It is important that history doesn't continue to divide Poles forever," he has told me often enough. I believe that to try him or not was a major dilemma, because it had to do with the attitude of your society toward the Communist past in general. Seeing that there was no consensus on how to proceed, your office dragged its feet until very recently. After all, life is what happens precisely in between these (or any other) two extremes. Again, as the General himself said: "History and the question of who is right are complicated and cannot be seen in terms of black and white."

I am sure that you, Sir, with your experience in such matters, would agree with me that truth and justice are brother and sister—but sometimes it is hard to maintain an equilibrium between them without causing even more harm to society. After all, a courtroom should deal not with moral issues, but with individual guilt proved by evidence. The important question in the General's case is: What values do you want to promote: retaliation or social consensus; further conflict or reconciliation? That is my understanding, although Napoleon claims that this trial has nothing to do with either truth or justice, but only politics. Well, perhaps he overheard somebody saying this; I cannot imagine that he deduced it on his own . . .

The General is, as they say in the media, a "divisive figure" in Polish society. There is no doubt about the controversy he has been provoking for almost two decades now, long before I was even born. (Please note, Mr. Prosecutor, that I am being very honest with you, to the point of even admitting my age, which a lady cat should never do!) So, the controversy, which everybody knows about by now, is that the General claims he declared martial law in order to save Poland from Soviet invasion. In short, he saved lives in an act of patriotism. For twenty years, the General has been consistently defending his decision: "We were threatened with fratricidal conflict, and we could have inflicted on ourselves incalculable tragedy."

Today, in spite of this controversy, the General's public standing is better than the president's brothers'! For years, opinion polls about whether the Poles believe his justification for martial law have been roughly split down the middle, suggesting that at least one half of Poland's citizens accept it. They don't think that it is necessary to put the General on trial. After all, although most Poles did not choose to live under Communism, they just went along and lived under Communism, accepting the military regime as reality. It is not in their interest to go back and wash their own dirty linen. The other half of Poles, however, would like to "purify" society of its Communist remnants. They prefer a fresh start, a sharp division between past and present, between totalitarianism and democracy. For such *purists*, Poland was divided into Communist supporters and the opposition, with nothing in between. To them, the trial of the General represents an act of revenge. "A traitor is not a victim of circumstances," they say. But this is a moral statement, and it is not helpful with the trial. I personally would hesitate to belittle the possibility that the General was acting out of patriotism—but I might be prejudiced about him. Because I ask myself, Does the fact that he was a Communist exclude his patriotism? I think not.

"Down with the enemy!" barks Napoleon incongruently when I—out of sheer pity—tell him about the pros and cons of the trial. Sometimes, as an intellectual, I do feel the responsibility of keeping him informed. But what can such a poor creature think when I ask him, Who are *them*? except that I am showing off.

The truth about the General is that he did indeed

proclaim martial law on December 13, 1981. The truth is that, as a consequence, the Solidarity movement was banned, its members were persecuted and jailed, censorship was introduced, freedom suspended, and fifty-six people were killed in the year that followed—that is all true. The General does not dispute any of this. The truth is also that in his political career, he made other wrong decisions that inflicted pain upon the Poles. Even when he was not acting on his own but as a member of the ruling political elite—for example, when dispatching Polish troops to Prague in 1968 as part of the Warsaw Pact invasion. Or when there was the shooting in Gdansk in 1970 in which forty-four protesters were killed. The truth is that he was a political leader who had accumulated too many functions (prime minister, minister of defense, president, head of the Military Council of National Salvation), logically leading him to assume dictatorial power.

I understand all this. Maybe this is the moment to stress again that I am sentimental, that I would like to defend the General. However, while I am on his side in my heart, I try to keep a clear head: I don't want to defend him from the truth—blind faith is his dog's defining trait, not mine.

Sir, before I take you any further, you should bear in mind my special position. I have a chance to observe the General from a very privileged perspective, being the one who sits in his lap most often. Napoleon is too big. And, thank God, we don't keep horses in the house yet, except in pictures. So, he caresses me. He speaks to me. He trusts me, I would say. You see, I am small and elegant, and I try not to be obtrusive. Sometimes I purr, just to make him feel good. Usually I simply sit there quietly in order to watch and listen. Like any "real" psychiatrist would.

He is bony, and to sit in his lap is not very comfortable, to say the least. But boy, is he warm, and that counts for a lot when you are not so young yourself. And he strokes me, which I found out is good for my back. He does it somewhat absentmindedly, because he does it while he reads, and he reads a lot, or listens to the news on the radio—he almost never watches TV—in his small studio on the first floor of the house. I let him do it—I mean, rub me and read at the same time. You can't take away all the fun from an old man, now can you? It wouldn't be nice of me. Meanwhile, I ponder subjects of my interest . . .

My real interest is not politics, it's psychology. Being, well, a semiprofessional, in human terms, I don't judge people. You may think that I need to study the psyche of the General because I depend upon his will. Or because I need to know my enemy. I would not go that far; the General is a good cat-keeper. He does not taunt me with bizarre little dangling objects, as other humans do. I get far better treatment than Napoleon, who is extremely jealous of my privileged position, grumbling stupidly that it is not fair. As if life were fair! In return, I listen and try to understand the General. I also try to understand humans as such, with their strengths and weaknesses. I am essentially fond of your kind of primate! I find you as a species interesting, often puzzling, mostly not very intelligent—but worth observing. You perhaps do not fully trust the observations of a feline psychiatrist without adequate formal education? But please consider that I am in a position to closely scrutinize how human beings behave for the simple reason that *I do nothing but observe them full-time*.

Now, I am well aware that you might harbor a certain suspicion that I am subjective, i.e., prejudiced in favor of my keeper. But let me assure you that my subjective feelings do not stand in the way of my professional findings about the said human being. On the contrary, I treat him like any other patient of mine, like, for example, his wife (a very nice lady, loved by her students!) and his darling only daughter. The pet daughter! Yet, there is no competition between the two of us—she has far too little time and patience for the old man . . . No, I am certainly able to keep the necessary distance between the object of my study and myself. In fact, the General doesn't even know that I am writing this letter. I had to do it behind his back, because he would strongly disapprove of it, maybe even scold me. I only worry that Napoleon, in his simplicity, might bark something to him. But he barks pretty incomprehensibly, and the General is a bit deaf, so I am not really nervous about it.

Please allow me to make a digression here. I am afraid that I have to use this opportunity to make you aware of an injustice in your domain. I am convinced that I qualify as a character witness at the General's trial. I personally volunteered to tell the court that he is a good man. I have sent enough obvious signs of my intention. I also sent a letter to the judge. Believe it or not, the response I received was rejection on the grounds of my species! A judge of the criminal court rejected me as a character witness with these words: "We hereby inform you that, as a rule, our court does not accept witnesses of alien origin." First and foremost, I am not an "alien." *E.T. is an alien.* I am a cat! Disregarding this display of ignorance on the part of the said judge, where does your law make this stipulation? He did not even bother to cite the clause that would forbid me to testify, a grave mistake for someone who is responsible for the law.

I ask you now, Sir, who is really harboring prejudices here, not to use the word discrimination or even racism for the view expressed by the judge? Should I have responded by demonstrating exactly the same kind of prejudice toward your own species and saying that he is only a *primate*!? I do have my feline pride, you know (although, as I mentioned before, some call it arrogance)! If this judge of yours were a true Polish gentleman in the first place, he would never have allowed himself to offend a lady.

But let us put this distasteful issue aside. After all, I am not the subject of this letter. I feel that it is my duty to tell you more about the General. So, let me tell you now, if I may, about the crucial moment in the General's life, about the moment of his decision of December 1981.

"Listen, Gorby," he told me one evening in that agitated mood that sometimes overcomes him. "People should believe me that there was no other way; I did not have a choice in December 1981. It really was a matter of the lesser evil, as is often the case in politics. You, of all creatures, know how rarely I speak about that part of my life . . . I do not like to remember those moments—you call it suppression, no? Oh, if only you had been there, in Moscow on that December night when the Soviet comrades summoned me to a meeting of the Politburo, for 'consultations,' as they called it. I still remember the tense, nervous atmosphere in the room. Leonid Brezhnev was sitting at the head of a long table with his bulldog face and beady eyes. He was already very ill, but no less dangerous for it. And Andropov was breathing down his neck. These comrades looked to me like a pack of dangerous dogs, ready to bite. Not much was said, but from their looks

I understood the precarious situation Poland was in, with the Solidarity movement's demands undermining the entire Communist system. They were afraid that the 'Polish pestilence'—as one of them put it—would spread if it was not 'contained.' That reminded me of 1968, of the moment when we in Poland were forced to send our soldiers against our brothers in Prague. How I regret that today! And how sadly it ended there, how we crushed Dubček and his reforms!

"It should have been clear to me then what was clear to Brezhnev in 1981: that Communism was not a system that could be reformed, and that any such attempt would only bring it down. Gorbachev did not understand that either, unbelievable as it sounds. When, almost two decades later, it was Gorbachev's turn to try reform—how did it end? With the collapse of almost the entire Communist world. I admire that man for his brave attempt to do the impossible—but I do not understand why he didn't learn from the failure of the 'Prague Spring' and from martial law in Poland? Was he so naïve? Or just a hard-core believer in Communism, like me?

"Anyhow, in 1981 Brezhnev was not naïve at all. He forced me to act, because he knew what we did not. There was no question of the Soviets leaving us in peace to slowly reform our Communism as we saw fit. They did not want another Aleksander Dubček. As Brezhnev-the-bulldog told me in no uncertain terms in his office before the meeting with the others: 'How long do you intend to tolerate anarchy? Either you take care of your problems, or else we will.' His words were not open to interpretation, my friend. He did not suggest that, for example, I should resign if I didn't curb the protests or something as benign as that. It would have been an easy choice; I would have gladly done it. True, he never said what his threat really meant; he never mentioned the words 'military intervention'—in that my opponents are right. The Soviet threat was never spelled out! However, there was not the slightest doubt as to what Brezhnev and all the rest really had in mind.

"You probably wonder if I was afraid. Later people asked me, did I feel physically threatened. I fought in the Second World War, Gorby. I know what fear is. No, this was not the fear of death that one feels in war. All soldiers feel it; it's only human. But when you are fighting, there is a certain moment when fear turns into indifference. Or, better said, into a reconciliation with one's destiny, acceptance of the consequences. You cannot fight and be afraid all the time. Therefore, you have to make peace with yourself—perhaps not consciously. I believe it is the survival instinct that makes us acknowledge death in order to live. What a beautiful contradiction, when you think of it!

"I remember I went to the men's room. There was a mirror there. I looked at myself. I felt calm, just like in 1943 when I was sure I would be killed by the

Germans in a battle. So, then and there, in the toilet of the Kremlin palace, I made my decision: Poland would be saved from invasion! I was ready to sacrifice my reputation rather than the lives of my people. Let me make this clear to you: I was well aware of the price I would personally have to pay for such a decision, and, as my mother would say, I was ready to bear my cross. But back then I thought that one day, when the crisis of Communism was over (imagine how trusting I was!), my people would realize that my decision had been necessary in order to save their lives. Back in the conference room I told our Soviet comrades that they need not worry; we Poles would take care of our 'problems' ourselves. I could not, of course, repeat the word 'pestilence.' Brezhnev stood up, slapped me on my back, and grinned unpleasantly. That was it."

This is what the General himself confessed to me. Therefore, the problem of this trial, as I see it now, is that it will be his word against those who say that there was no Soviet invasion planned. Indeed, lately even some documents were found in support of this. But who could have known that then?

To all this I could add a few conclusions about his character: The General is a serious person. You rarely see a photo of him smiling, only in family photos perhaps. Usually he is somber, his dark glasses adding to his gloom, showing that he carries a heavy weight on his shoulders. Although he is not without a sense of humor! He is a man of principles, even if these principles are different from yours or mine. As an illustration, I will only tell you that he did not enter the church at the funeral of his mother, an ardent Catholic. No, not even in plain clothes. He waited in front of the church until the service was over. *"A Communist army general does not go to church under any circumstances!"* he told me later on. Even if you don't believe this anecdote, I can vouch that for him duty is above all else. This—permit me to say—is not a very catholic value. Besides, he proved to be intelligent and capable of grasping the new situation and adapting to it. A complex personality . . . Which is precisely my reason for writing this letter, in my capacity as both a specialist in human psychology and his friend. Do I even need to tell you that Napoleon, when I told him about my intention to write this letter, dismissed it sneeringly, calling you "a bloodsucker"? But that is his level, I am afraid.

In spite of his—not my!—low opinion of you, Sir, I would like to trust you. I already said that my name is Gorby, after Gorbachev. I am well aware that you—like many others before you—might be puzzled by my name. The General himself gave it to me, although, considering my female gender, it would have been more appropriate, wouldn't it, to have named me Raisa, after Gorby's wife, whom he loved so dearly. It seems like a paradoxical twist that the General (my pet human) should name his pet cat after somebody who dismantled Communism and therefore should be his enemy. But, believe me, he had his reasons. He admired Gorby—almost like Napoleon (the man, not the dog, of course). The mere fact that he named me after Gorby should tell you a lot about the General himself.

The great absurdity of Gorby's life (not mine!) was that *the collapse of Communism was the result of his own attempt to reform it*, to perfect it, as he himself said. Isn't that a sad destiny, to live to see exactly the opposite of what you intended? To have the whole world admire you for something that you did not want to achieve? To see people applaud you for the mistake you made? In hindsight it looks like a comedy, but it is a tragedy! So, they *both believed in the possibility of saving Communism*, one way or another, and they both ended up losers. Gorby is almost like a character from a comedy of errors. Think about it: The outstanding political change of the twentieth century happened, in fact, by mistake!

Gorby was, no doubt, a believer. The General was a believer, too. "A faith is not acquired by reasoning . . . Reason may defend an act of faith—but only after the act has been committed, and the man committed to the act," wrote Arthur Koestler. I think that for the General—as for many other believers—the main problem was the difference between theory and practice: Obviously, for him, in theory Communism looks good. So let us suppose, for the sake of argument, that you are a true Communist (you acquired a faith) who early enough became aware of the "deviations" in practice. You are part of the power structure. You think that you could do better. What do you do? You reach for, shall we say, unethical means in order to achieve your aim. You act brutally in order to save your beloved Poland from the invasion, in accordance with the principle of the end justifying the means. That is, you make a pact with the devil, in this case, Moscow. But—and this is not an excuse, only a clarification—you act as a man of faith. Later on you understand what the consequences of what you have done are and you regret it—only, it is too late. Can you be redeemed? Do you deserve pity? Well, that depends upon the circumstances, I suppose you would say.

In both my feline—that is, subjective—and professional views, the General is perhaps an even more tragic person than Gorbachev. He lost the battle to improve Communism by ruthless means and *destroyed his moral credibility*, which was not the case with Gorbachev. The General is tragic for another reason, too: because he has admitted publicly that he was defeated. He claims that he believes Communism failed, that he is now a social democrat, and, moreover, that he likes Poland as it is today. Yet, *he has never repented for martial law*! He has never admitted that his decision to impose it was wrong. On the contrary, he still maintains that it was a necessary measure to save Poland . . . In other words, the General did not do the single, most important thing that would have saved him from being put on trial: He did not repent for his decision. And that is unforgivable—at least for half of the Polish citizens. He is not to be forgiven for standing up for his belief. He has to pay for his sins!

This attitude, in the time of a moral decay, is, you have to admit, rather brave, I'd say.

Napoleon comments, "Your justice in just a few words: an eye for an eye." Being a cat, I don't trust dogs, and I can't believe in such primitivism on the part of democratic Poland. Please, Sir! I am aware that I sound pathetic now, but the General must be given a chance to redeem himself. In your religion, everyone must be given this chance. You must have considered whether there is something to say in his defense. Correct me if I am wrong, but it was the General who made possible the first free elections that Solidarity won. You could claim that, in a way, he was forced to the roundtable talks in the spring of 1989—or to invite Solidarity to enter the coalition government. He also stepped down from the presidency. The General considers Solidarity's later triumph to have been made possible by the decisions he made during and after the imposition of martial law.

However, something like a Solidarity-generation complex still runs very deep in this society. I mean that participants in the roundtable negotiations with the General are themselves being treated as traitors. Politics is the art of compromise, and compromise (enabled by the General) brought about the change of power. Yet political compromise, dialogue, and consensus—even if they played a great role in the nineties—are not sufficiently part of this culture. This is not difficult to understand in view of the past: What could you humans learn about compromise when you were living in a totalitarian society? But this complicates the case of the General even more . . .

I know, Mr. Prosecutor, that justice is needed, but I ask you: What is justice in the case of the General? Going back to where I started: Does he really have to be tried in a criminal court like an ordinary criminal or Mafioso? Are you sure that this trial will satisfy the principle of justice? Some authorities in the field of law, for example, have expressed their doubts that the charges stand. Is the trial going to be useful—or maybe even harmful to the society? The General himself is not opposing a trial, because it gives him yet another chance to say what he considers to be the truth in his own words, since he cares about his role in history and he wants to set the record straight.

Napoleon, predictably, unquestioningly believes every word the General says. He is, you know, very much a soldier type. I, on the other hand, think that my duty as a feline intellectual is to ask the right questions. The main question is, What is the purpose of this trial? Is it to achieve symbolic justice, or is it a case of belated retribution? Is he being tried as a person or as a symbol? Formally he was put on trial for illegally imposing martial law. It is expected to be a ritual of exorcising the evil spirit of Communism and, as such, to help society mentally step out of its past. In that sense, perhaps it would be wise to hold a trial. But if you are honest, you must admit that, so far, this looks like an act of revenge for decades of Communist rule, no more and no less. Vengeance, however, is a bad motive. Your office should not take part in something like that. What would you achieve? Are you sure that you are not looking for a scapegoat, not knowing how to deal with the problematic past?

Besides, it should be taken into consideration that the General has expressed regret for the pain his decision has brought to many of his fellow humans. I do not need to remind you, of all human beings, that only a person with an ethical code could do that. This is no small matter. "I am sorry. I regret mainly the social costs of this dramatically difficult decision and those cases where particular people suffered," he said. A man needs to be a strong character to be able to say this, you have to give him that!

Now, I am not asking the victims to forgive the General; I merely believe that it is important for a society to be able to demonstrate mercy. Polish society is as tolerant and wise as the mercy it can bestow upon humans like the General. Why am I calling for mercy? Because, in my opinion, it would be important for this society to realize that the General was defeated long ago—and one does not beat a dead horse. In his case, would it not be better to demonstrate some benevolence and let him continue to live in moral condemnation instead? Politically, he has already been a loser for twenty years now. Leave the final sentence to history. In doing so, you would show the compassionate side of the Polish government and society in whose name you act. I remember what Adam Michnik, the dissident imprisoned under the General with whom I tend to agree, once said about the whole affair of the trial: "It's a subject for historians, writers, priests, moralists, and confessors, not for the courts."

On the other hand (because there is always the other side to consider in such matters), there is an argument that says: The tribunal in Nuremberg did more to pronounce Nazism than generations of historians . . .

But there is something else that worries me, too. To prosecute the General in a criminal court is simply an act to humiliate that person. Moreover, by humiliating the General, the Poles would be humiliating themselves, too. They would be spitting on forty-five years of their own past, their own lives—like two people after a bitter divorce. Perhaps that is one of the reasons why so many Poles accept his justification of martial law as a "lesser evil"? The others, those who insist on his trial, however, perhaps believe that all *their* sins would be redeemed once the sentence was passed—as if the General were Jesus. Does this sound like a metaphor to you? A literary gimmick of mine? Well, I love literature, but this is not the case here. No, in the case of the General, *redemption is the cultural matrix* we are looking at in this society, Catholic to its core. Redemption of their Communist sins would come in very handy, because it would divest them of their own responsibility. Was the General the only one to blame for martial law? No, there were thousands and hundreds of thousands who aided and abetted military rule for more than a decade. What about them? Not every Pole was a member of the Solidarity movement. Once the General is sentenced, others can wash their hands.

In saying all this, what am I actually proposing for you to do?

First and foremost, I ask you to make your decision quickly, whatever it might be. I am not suggesting you suspend the trial, although clearly I would prefer this solution as the wisest. I think I have presented my arguments for this option, but you may find them inadequate and decide for the trial to go on. If so, please, do it! But order the court to proceed quickly. The General is an old and very frail man. In my opinion, if you don't speed it up, he has no chance of seeing the end of the trial. It is my worst nightmare that he will die before the trial is over. Of course I would be devastated by his passing; I am his pet after all. But his death would present society with another problem: If you allow it to happen, there won't be any closure for society—and that is what is expected of his trial, to close the chapter on Communism. You know what happened with the Slobodan Milošević case in the Hague? Not that I compare these two; in my opinion there is no comparison between the General—a tragic believer in Communism who made a pact with the devil in good faith—and an opportunistic manipulator, a thug, and a war criminal. Milošević died way before his trial was over. And because of that, the Serbs were never confronted with their responsibility for the wars in the Balkans. Denial rules in Serbia today; it is as if he and his murderous nationalist politics were never on trial. No truth, no justice, no closure or catharsis . . . nothing.

For the sake of Poland, I would like you to avoid this happening here! Your responsibility is great and I urge you to be aware of it. Even Napoleon agrees with me on this, although I am not sure that he understands the problem at all.

With this appeal, I salute you in the hope that you will not disregard my letter just because I was fortunate enough to be born a cat, and not a human being.

V

THE LEGEND OF THE BERLIN WALL— AS PRESENTED BY A MOLE

Dear Members of the Learned Society, Distinguished Guests,

Many, many generations of Moles ago, near the place where we are right now, there stood a massive concrete structure called the Berlin Wall. The well-known Mole Legend tells us that it was erected at several periods during ancient times, starting in *anno domini* 1961. When it was finished in *anno domini* 1975, it was 3.6 meters high and 140 kilometers long. As a collector of old Legends, and being interested in archaeology, I was curious to find out how much truth (if any) this Legend contained. For example, I find it particularly interesting that Men used to dig tunnels under this very Wall, as if they were Moles themselves. Was this only an invention of our ancestors? Apparently one such tunnel is said to have been 145 meters long—an admirable achievement and length, even by our standards. A Mole like me would need some seven to ten days to dig it, but then it would not be 70 centimeters high, as this one supposedly was. We Moles don't need such high passages, as we would call them, because, quite obviously, we are much smaller than Men. Also, it was not the habit of us Moles to "escape" from one side of the then existing Wall to the other, which, according to the Legend, was evidently what triggered the digging of the tunnel in the first place. Living in the Underland, even then we Moles used to move everywhere, politely greeting our neighbors from what Men from the Overland used to call the "Other Side." Of course, we never cared much about their different sides, but while investigating this part of the Legend about the tunnel, I slowly came to realize why they did. Men did not descend into our world without a reason.

Why did this long tunnel fascinate us Moles? I guess that we Underland creatures felt some kind of solidarity, even pity, because to dig with clumsily built bodies and without proper tools to make up for such a shortcoming must have been an exhausting job. Moles are by nature equipped for such work; we have paws adapted for digging. But poor Men must rely upon various kinds of substitute paws, like shovels and a variety of frightening, noisy machines that—for the very specific reason of secrecy—were not available to those who dug the legendary tunnel under the Wall. It had to be dug by hand, and therefore our forefathers must have felt sorry and tried to help Men by digging in front of them, making the soil more porous—or so the Legend goes.

Allegedly, Men started to dig this tunnel in *anno domini* 1964, soon after the Berlin Wall was erected. Except that it was not a concrete Wall right away, but a wall made out of barbed wire. As you know, normally, when we hear people digging, we run away. They produce vibrations that are very disturbing to us. Since we don't see very well, we are very oversensitive to sounds. We are used to silence, and to the ordinary sounds of Overland life, which we experience as a dull and hushed noise. But on that occasion the sound of their digging was almost as inaudible as ours—although, in my experience, Men are too prone to chat—and the Moles were hardly disturbed by it. I guess that our old ones were grateful for that. If I remember correctly what I was told as a youngster, and I believe that I do, the entrance into the tunnel was in a backyard toilet in the then Eastern part of Berlin. One had to descend to a depth of twelve meters! The exit hole was in the cellar of a former bakery in Bernauer Strasse, situated on the Western side. My grandma told me she heard that Moles from the surroundings would come together in order to marvel at the diggers and their commitment, while they were busy filling push-carts with earth and then taking them up to the cellar and emptying them there. According to these Moles, it took the diggers six long months to accomplish this admirable job!

It was particularly tough when the tunnel was finished and the first few people went down in order to make their "escape." If they are not miners, Men do not go down to the Underland, and when they must, their first reaction is to panic. We know that feeling from another kind of experience—from ending up there in the Overland by mistake. It happened to me once when I thrust my head out in the wrong place—actually, in an excavation in the middle of a street with heavy traffic. I just popped out for a moment, and was immediately blinded by sunlight and deafened by the sounds of the passing cars. I still remember what a shock it was; it took me days to recover from it. I imagine that these Men descending to our Underland must have felt something similar. Passing through that tunnel must have been an extremely traumatic experience for every single one of them. Men in general are very dependent upon their eyesight; in the tunnel they could not see anything, so they had to carry some sort of light-casting device. They were afraid of suffocating, and their hearts were beating too fast. In some places they had to crawl almost like snakes, which to Moles witnessing the scene must have looked funny. There is a story about one old Man, probably the oldest in the group, who evidently suffered from claustrophobia. He fainted and had to be carried back to the toilet. But in spite of this unpleasant accident, he tried once more and succeeded, so big was his wish to leave. Another person had a heart problem and, in the middle of the tunnel, had an attack and thought that he would die there, underground. He started to yell and cry. Others in the group were petrified, fearing that guards posted along the Wall to prevent just such events would hear him. As they had advanced too far and there was no way back (Too risky? Too complicated? I do not know, but it was impossible for this reason or another.) one of the escapees put his hand over the sick Man's mouth to prevent him from yelling. He almost killed his suffering companion. Evidently, the escapees were ready to sacrifice this unfortunate person's life in order to save the group. If their attempt to escape had been discovered, they would have all gone to jail for many years.

In order to fully comprehend this part of the Legend, one has to know that in ancient times these Men living in the Overland were ruled by a great fear of guards and all kinds of uniformed people, as well as Men without uniforms but in powerful positions. To "escape"—i.e., to migrate without permission from the Supreme Authority called the State—was considered a grave and highly punishable offense. However, there were rumors that a certain number of Men managed to obtain such permission and could leave legally, but most of them were old and sick. The Legend does not deal with this specific issue in more detail, but it seems that they were exported just because of the reasons mentioned. It is hard to guess why the Other Side would have wanted Men in such condition if not to demonstrate its charitable intentions. But if these specific categories of Men could have served some other unknown and unimaginable purpose, this knowledge is lost now.

There were thousands of specially trained soldiers and dogs posted all along the Wall. There were 116 watchtowers in order to prevent any attempts at escape, which were anyway numerous. On this point the legend is amazingly specific: some 5,000 men managed to make it to the other side, while 72,000 were jailed for trying to escape. But there is still, to this very day, a dispute about the number of killed escapees, and various versions speak of either one hundred or two hundred. Still, because most Men were not free to leave that Overland country, they feared the police more than the soldiers posted at the Wall. In particular, they feared a kind of secret policeman whose job was to spy on ordinary Men committing any kind of "subversion" (?!) and report on them to the same Supreme Authority. Such spies were called Stasi, and their particular quality was that they were numerous and looked just like ordinary Men, so that you couldn't tell one from the other. Consequently, as our ancestors noticed, the biggest fear of the escapees in the legendary tunnel was that one of these Stasi might infiltrate their group. Or, perhaps one of 189,000 of their "informal employees." I must say I do not believe that there could really have been such imminent danger. This looks more like a picturesque addition to the Legend, as it is hard to believe that a Man would go into a tunnel with the sole intention of spying. Incidentally, I also learned that Men use the term "Mole" to describe such a double agent—that is, a person pretending to be a member of the group of escapees while actually working for the police. Needless to say, dear colleagues, I find that usage highly inappropriate, if not insulting.

The Legend of the Berlin Wall lives on because we Moles remembered it and passed it on to our children as a cautionary tale about how strangely Men could behave and how little we know about them. But there are some questions raised in connection with this remarkable endeavor. It seems puzzling why these Men, exactly fifty-seven of them, were so desperate to risk their lives in order to reach the cellar of a former bakery. What was hidden there? Clearly, the answer had to do with the Wall. But why was the Wall there in the first place? I mean, those two walls, of course. Because we tend to forget that there were two Berlin Walls, although the Legend mentions only that the second one was erected later on—with a strip of land in between tellingly called the "Death Strip." It was deadly only for Men, of course, because according to some versions, there was wildlife there, such as rabbits, mice, birds, and insects, even cats, not to mention our own population. It is said that in those days we even used to mate there. Although safety is al-

ways our first priority, we could easily disappear into the Underland in the case of shooting. Unlike Men, for example. Or
rabbits, for that matter.

Why that second, parallel Wall was built was something we
pondered over for generations. As if one single such construction would not have been enough to prevent people from crossing over? We know that Men are great builders; they like to
build all sorts of structures. We therefore assume they built that
gigantic Wall in order to protect themselves from their powerful
enemies. But even from our underground perspective one could
tell that, in their case, there could be no other, more dangerous
predators threatening them. It would be strange to have built a
Wall for reasons of security. Man is a species without natural
enemies, a quite remarkable fact when you come to think about
it. Therefore, my hypothesis was (and later you will see why I
am using the past tense here) that these two Walls, separated
by a strip of wasteland some one hundred meters wide, had no
other logical purpose but to divide their hunting territory.
"The two walls must have been there because of hunting," I
thought.

Now, what on earth—or, as we Moles would say, what
under earth!—was there on the Other Side? What kind of trea-
sure did they want to hunt so eagerly?

In the middle of my research I met Andreas, an elderly, learned
Mole who lives in what used to be the West side; as you are aware,
for several generations there have formally been no sides. He happened to be the proper person to address some questions to about
ancient habits in that part of the Overland. Andreas, of course,

was acquainted with the Legend. "Tell me, please," I asked, "have you found indications of why some people from the East side of the Wall wanted to go to the West?" He looked a bit surprised by my question. "Well, Tillman, have you never heard of the banana issue!?" I had to admit that I was not aware of that aspect of the Legend (by the way, it looked less and less like a Legend to me, the deeper I dug into it). And no—I had never heard about bananas. "What are bananas?" I asked Andreas. "They are a delicacy. You should imagine a banana as an exquisite, extremely succulent, tasty kind of earthworm. Even the mere mentioning of bananas makes Men's mouth water," he said. "Oh, I do understand that, the mere thought of a special kind of fat earthworm—and my favorite ones are *megadriles* from the *Tubificidae* family—makes my mouth water as well!" I exclaimed, happy to have learned something new.

In the old days, before the Berlin Wall went down, bananas were a very popular food among Men. "But in those days," Andreas continued, "unlike other popular foods, there was something particular about bananas. While on the West side of the Wall (the banana side, so to speak) Men did not especially appreciate them, probably because they could indulge in them every day; on the nonbanana side they were literally dying for them." Then he explained to me something crucial: The Men who did not appreciate such fine food enough all lived *within the Wall*—they were, so to speak, walled-in in West Berlin. In other words, during ancient times Berlin was a kind of prison, albeit a luxury one with plenty of *megadriles*—I mean, bananas! Bananas seemed to abound there, as they were sent to the prison from somewhere else, where the prisoners' kinfolk lived. "But it doesn't make sense that Men in a prison should have such good food like bananas, while those outside, who surely had more access to hunting, would be prepared to risk their lives in order to get it," I remarked to Andreas. "Well, dear Tillman, don't forget that we are dealing here with human affairs, strange to us already by definition," he reminded me.

After this meeting I decided to look more profoundly into the enigma of bananas. I had a premonition that it might be the key to understanding why the Wall had been built. So I looked here and there and found out from varied sources that at that time bananas were so important that Men even cracked so-called banana jokes. The most popular one goes like this: Two Berliner children are speaking to each other over the Wall (but let me remark here that this was hardly possible; the Wall was much too high!). The little boy in the West says, while eating a banana, "Look, I have a banana." The boy in the East answers: "Yes, but we have socialism!" The boy in the West counters: "We, too, will have socialism soon." But the boy in the East says triumphantly: "Tough luck, then; you won't have bananas anymore!"

Obviously, you had either bananas or "socialism"; the two of them didn't grow together. But what was this *socialism*? "Another kind of food?" I asked myself. Based on available sources, I soon came to the conclusion that socialism must have been not food but a kind of pestilence that prevented bananas from growing in the Eastern part of the Overland.

I have to admit that the Legend about the Berlin Wall is still cryptic and confusing concerning some crucial points. But, as Andreas would say, so is most of what goes on in the Overland. In trying to think logically about this enigma of bananas—and logic is what we Moles care most about—it seemed that Men on the nonbanana side of the Wall (although I have to remind myself it would be proper to use the plural here) did everything in their rather limited power to reach the banana side. To achieve that aim they had to fight both an internal enemy, such as fear, as well as external ones, i.e., guards and the Stasi. The reason for this seems to be that Men were going crazy about these fantastic and—due to the pestilence—rare earthworms. Again, if I were to pursue a Mole's line of reasoning, I would have to conclude that Men built the Wall(s) in order to protect themselves from that pestilence called socialism that was on the Eastern side. But the Legend tells us just the opposite! Those who built the Wall(s) were those marked by pestilence and the lack of bananas—so what were they protecting?

After having pondered a while, I thought that there could be only one answer: The Men on the nonbanana side built the Wall(s) to protect the prisoners and bananas from socialism. They surely demonstrated extraordinary care for the others, a noble characteristic of human beings. Regrettably, I cannot claim that we Moles would have done the same.

Then I had to look for Andreas again, as the two of us had another logical problem to solve. "If the building of the Berlin Wall(s) was really a protective measure against pestilence, as I believe it was, why would somebody infected by socialism try to escape *into* the prison, risking infecting the prisoners? Would that not be extremely irresponsible behavior? By the way, I suppose this banana hunt is the only known case of a population trying to break into a prison, not *out* of one," I told him. But this time he was not very helpful. "There is not much hope that a Mole—that logical, rational creature—would ever be able to completely understand irrational, emotional, confused human beings and their deeds, Tillman," Andreas nodded. I was not satisfied with such an abstract answer. "Isn't it bizarre that prisoners on the banana side claimed that they were free, while those on the nonbanana side tried to jump over the Wall(s), or crawl under them, just because of their wish to move and eat freely within the prison? Again, here we have the unique case of prisoners claiming they feel free," I insisted.

"It is not as bewildering as you believe," Andreas said. "Imagine that you live in a territory you call a prison, but you have the possibility to get out of it if you wish, passing through— never mind how!—a tiny strip of land in the foreign territory populated by the enemy. You are not a prisoner because you can leave whenever you want. Isn't that so?" "Yes, indeed," I had to admit. "West Berlin was such a place," Andreas said. "Although half the city was within foreign territory, it was still connected to a bigger, free one." He did not explain any more about that free world, but it was a bit clearer to me why Men wanted to escape and ended up first in the prison, which was not a prison because, in the strict sense of the word, you could leave it by certain restricted routes. "And what were they searching for even beyond that West Berlin prison?" I asked Andreas. "More succulent earthworms, of course!" he replied.

After that I had no other option but to conclude that, in these ancient times of the Wall(s), what Men defined as freedom was moving from one banana place to another.

In my further research into this Legend, which more and more seemed to me to be based upon at least some historical facts, I learned that, indeed, there are further proofs of the strange behavior of Men. I mean, material evidence that cannot be disputed. For example, Men had other means of getting out of the nonbanana part of Berlin, not only through tunnels as I had thought at the beginning. They would also fly off in a bird-like machine. Or escape in a fishlike machine, if one preferred diving to flying. I heard from one Mole, who knows a Mole, who knows another Mole who heard about a Man flying such a machine, which resembles an eagle (we know a bit about that cursed marauder, the archenemy of our rabbit friends). Starting from a far-off banana place, he landed in a field in the nonba-nana Overland. There his sweetheart was waiting for him. He grabbed her, as an eagle would have grabbed an unlucky Mole, and flew away with her into the sunset—as Men would prob-ably have put it poetically. Presumably, they lived happily ever after, but this supposition belongs more to the realm of fairy tales, not to my research.

Then something occurred that made me completely change my mind about what the Legend is and what the real story is, i.e., history.

One of my acquaintances was recently snooping in the cor-ridors of a huge dwelling near where the Wall(s) used to stand. Knowing my interest in the topic, and especially knowing my archaeological inclination, he reported to me that there he had seen a place with a lot of artifacts that ought to interest me. "A very educational place," my acquaintance said. "That is why so many Men come to see it, presumably to learn how to escape." Well, out of sheer politeness I did not comment upon his con-clusion, although it crossed my mind to tell him how wrong it was to say such a thing. Where would Men escape to now, when the Wall(s) no longer exist and the prison called West Berlin was abolished generations ago? But I kept quiet, because it was obvious that he was pretty uninformed about human affairs and their longing for freedom. Of course, I immediately went to that place myself. I was very excited about the possibility of seeing physical proofs that the Legend about the Wall(s) *was in fact not legend at all.*

Even if my intention is not to exaggerate, what I happened to see there was beyond belief. In short, I saw a whole collection of devices that Men in ancient times used to transport themselves from their free Overland to the desired Berlin prison. This collection proves the existence of the Wall(s) beyond any doubt. There were huge machines on wheels called trucks, which were used to crush the turnpike at the border crossing in Friedrichstrasse. And a homemade chairlift! A father sent his small son over the Wall(s) by using this invention. Unbelievable as it is, I also saw a hot-air balloon. Imagine, in *anno domini* 1979 two families escaped by using it to climb twenty-six hundred meters! There was a cable drum that smuggled people, too. I was also most impressed by ordinary cars. It was amazing how a gigantic creature, such as a grown-up male or female Man, could squeeze himself or herself into a small trunk, and thus became invisible to the border guards. One kind of car was built so low that it actually passed under the horizontal bar at the checkpoint, transporting three people. Even the tunnel I just told you about is documented there! That very place, called the Museum at Checkpoint Charlie, is in reality a *public registry of means for escape*. Now, by putting two and two together, I arrived at a definite conclusion: 1) the Wall(s) existed; 2) Men indeed tried to get from one side to the other; and 3) it mostly took place from the East side to the West. In the registry, at least, there is not a single documented case of a person escaping from the West to the East side of the Wall.

Last but not least, I also found out that a mysterious structure 1,316 meters long, called "the Monument" (?), that can be inspected even today at a specific location close to the river Spree—*is a remaining piece of the original Wall(s)*! This is perhaps the proper moment to thank you, dear colleagues, for your proposal that in our *Annals* I should be credited as the Mole who proved the Legend about the Berlin Wall(s) to be true. I am aware that this is a great honor and a big inspiration for my future work.

One could, of course, ask how it is possible that such an important place as the registry was not discovered before. As an explanation I can only say that chance and coincidence often play an immense role in the history of discoveries.

Looking further into this, now definitely a historical matter and not only a legend, I should add that I was also able to establish how the 140-kilometer-long Wall came down, except for that small part that remained standing. Logic would tell us that one day prisoners must have decided that they had had enough of their dull life. But, unfortunately, here we Moles are dealing with the particular—I'd dare say illogical—logic of Men, which means that it happened just the other way around: Those outside decided to invade the prison. Is it really possible that seventeen million souls were choosing to move into that rather tiny West Berlin? Yes, this seems to be what really happened. Men outside the prison—free Men on the East side of the Wall(s)—came to the unusual idea of escaping to the prison in order to lay claim to all the bananas! I know how strange it must seem to you, but (to paraphrase Andreas) it is typical of Men and their sudden and unpredictable changes of mood. Moreover, there are proofs that the prisoners agreed to this obvious plunder.

One day they all met at the top of one of the Walls (closer to the West) and embraced each other! On that memorable day, the ninth of November 1989, it is documented that they hugged each other and cried a lot. Although it is not clear to me why, it must have been such a happy occasion for everyone. As a result of that emotional, even hysterical (although it is called historical) meeting on top of the Wall, it seems likely that it simply collapsed under the weight of all these millions and millions of bodies. This must have been a very melodramatic event, with many victims, but—another surprise!—victims have not been mentioned at all. Maybe this was covered up on purpose, in order not to spoil the happy event. However, it is established that the happening was a very noisy one; a terrible thud could be heard in the whole Underland, and it scared to death many of our ancients. That might be yet another reason why the "Legend" about the Berlin Wall is remembered so vividly by so many generations of Moles.

We now know that the fatal meeting on the Wall, the one that made it collapse, was named "reunion." On that occasion, dignitaries from both sides signed the bilateral "Banana Treaty," which solved the problem once and for all, to everyone's satisfaction. Finally, seventeen million deprived inhabitants, not only from East Berlin but also from the whole free Overland, had achieved the right to consume bananas on equal terms with the (former) prisoners. No more need for tunnels or digging, flying or diving. No more need for Stasi interrogation rooms, about which some of our elders had told stories, although we considered them morbid fiction. And everybody from the West could enjoy the Staatsoper at Unter der Linden, the Pergamon Museum, the Hotel Adlon, and other fine institutions of the former nonbanana world.

Though, in light of the discovery that the Wall(s) existed it doesn't seem important, I continue to ponder over bananas. Where did all these bananas come from? And in such enormous quantities that everyone could eat them? This doesn't seem to have been a problem after the collapse. Newcomers to the banana world discovered that bananas grew in places called Supermarkets, together with an abundance of other fine foods, even finer than *megadriles* from the *Tubificidae* family— or whatever stands in for them in the Overworld. They soon discovered that the beauty of such Supermarkets consisted in the possibility of moving from one food item to another; you were even encouraged by posters called advertisements to do so. There were such enormous varieties of food there that, at the very beginning of their stay in the West, newcomers didn't even have names for some of them. There was a fine worm called caviar and another called cheese, and there was some very posh water with bubbles called Champagne, but it is hard to understand exactly why it excited Men so much. There were all kinds of dead animals in the shape of "prosciutto" or "salami," and lots of fine, dead fish and birds, and perhaps even nice tasty mice, caterpillars, and a crunchy grasshopper or two (but now I am daydreaming) . . .

However, Men would not be Men if they would not complicate their lives, as they are of a species not guided by *ratio*. Judging from their behavior it is clear that they are in constant need of supreme beings, some kind of super Men called Gods. This need is usually referred to as "religion." Traditionally, Gods are old Men with white beards who often claim to be invisible. It is, therefore, interesting to notice that the religion newcomers found on the banana side had nothing to do with these old, bearded, invisible Men. Rather, this particular type of religion was founded on an irresistible and therefore powerful (although foolish!) *desire to possess things*. And by this I don't mean only food—that would have been rational!—but *all sorts of things*. The newcomers learned that this ruling religion, the one they had not experienced before, was called "Consumerism." This was the big secret of the escapees, who had been ready to risk their lives in order to join its believers—a desire for bananas was only one aspect of it.

The newcomers came from the part of the Overland where religion of any kind was rather unpopular, if not forbidden. But in the former prison of West Berlin, churches of Consumerism were not forbidden at all. On the contrary, they were everywhere, situated along the main avenues as well as way out toward the periphery of settlements. They were brightly decorated, lit edifices, seductive in their appearances. To the admiration of newcomers, one could get everything in those huge churches (called Shopping Malls) celebrating Consumerism, anything at all *without even a prayer*. But there was kind of a trick that this religion played on its believers. They were free to enter a church but not to get out of it! From what we all know about religions in general, a person has to fulfill a set of rules in order to become a member of such a congregation. But in this case, it was (again!) just the opposite. This is how it works, and it has not changed, from November 9, 1989, to this day: Every Shopping Mall (as well as even the tiniest Supermarket) is supervised by slot machines called cash registers. These machines are positioned not at the entrance but at the very exit of the church. When a believer approaches the machine with a basket full of desired goods to quench his or her thirst for possessions, the machine scrutinizes the person in question. I imagine that the reason is to perform some sort of test of faith; it lets you pass and get out only if you are a true believer. That you have to demonstrate by either pushing a plastic card into the slot or by giving symbolic paper or metal tokens to the person, usually a female, sitting behind the cash register. Men who fail the test have to give back all the fabulous goodies they collected, and then they get very, very sad. Sometimes even uniformed assistants (lower priests?) come and take such persons away. To comfort them, I suppose. There is speculation that these tokens are so powerful that they could even be used to buy indulgences for sins, but this is hard to imagine. I would assume that, if sin exists, there must be a hell, and a paradise too, of which no proof has been found. Therefore, I assume such speculation must be unfounded.

I was also interested in what happened to the dangerous

pestilence called socialism (curiously enough, sometimes also called Communism, but I could not make out any substantial difference; this, however, in my opinion, deserves further clarification). Did not everyone get infected by it when the Wall(s) collapsed? Or was the world suddenly somehow miraculously cured of it? Well, first of all, soon after the invasion (or reunion), it turned out that *socialism was not a pestilence at all.* This was only a myth produced on the banana side, although it seemed to be true that bananas could not be obtained where socialism ruled. Socialism seems to have been a political, economic, and social order; its particular characteristics were lack of genuine elections and the aim to achieve equality of all Men but under the rule of only one. For example, before the time of the collapse of the Wall(s), that person was called Comrade Honecker. But everyone who lived during the period of socialism was called Comrade, so we could not be sure that this really was his first name. Comrade Honecker was well-known for kissing mouth-to-mouth with another old Man also called Comrade. You can see that even today on a painting on that remaining part of the Wall. It may well be that this was the habit of those days. I heard that Men call this way of kissing a life-saving method, and it is perfectly possible that elderly persons were saving each other's lives in this way; why not?

Anyhow, as it was not a pestilence, socialism could not have infected the entire Overland. The young generation of Men born after the collapse of the Wall(s) seems to know little about it or still believes (like us!) that it was only another Legend. But there are some from their grandparents' generation, and even their parents', who got sentimental and invented fairy tales about what allegedly used to be a "better life," times when equality ruled (equality or egalitarianism are the terms they seem to use for a lack of every kind of *megadrilles, haplotaxida*, i.e., food in general). Equality in hunger? In lack of bananas? This might seem absurd to you, but the doings and beliefs of Men should no longer surprise us. It is clear to me that they must have invented such tales for the very obvious reason that I described earlier, the fact that they were not qualified for the new church for lack of tokens.

Having arrived at the end of my presentation, it is perhaps important to add that I also found some artifacts connected to the political, economic, and social order that ruled on the other, i.e., Western, side of the Berlin Wall during those days. It was then, as it is still, called democracy. It means the governing of the *demos*, which is to say—in the Old Greek language that disappeared even before the Wall was built—the rule of the majority of Men. During the times of the Wall(s) there were rare individuals from the Eastern side who escaped to the Western side just because of love for democracy. I think it was appealing to Men because it was closely connected with an idea of freedom that had less to do with bananas and Consumerism than with so-called ideals. Today democracy governs in most of the Overland. However, I assume it must be hard to put it into practice. When I try to imagine such an order applied to us Moles, it looks to me like no decision could ever be taken, regardless of the beneficial result such an order would yield. I am therefore sure that there must be some technique unknown to us through which democracy can be efficiently applied. But all I managed to find out was that some Men had more power than others, although properly elected, and that they impose their power upon others from top to bottom, in a kind of pyramidal structure. But to tell the truth, they usually don't rule long. And it happens that even such an improved system as democracy, *sometimes* results in the rule of just one person, who then brings about a huge disaster called fascism. That happened a long, long time ago in the part of the Overland where we are now. In fact, we are holding our conference at the very same place where that particular Man—his name was Adolf Hitler—allegedly committed suicide because he could not bear his own defeat. He was defeated in the Big War by the united forces of banana and nonbanana countries, a fact as intriguing as it is puzzling. Needless to say, he must have been a weak character.

Still, in spite of this unfortunate event, Men must have considered the democratic system much better, as they almost completely abandoned socialism. Today most of them simply don't care about any political system or politics (this is what they call the fight for power to define the rules under which they live together). I dare say that nowadays they try to survive in a harsh world ruled not so much by Comrades or any other personality or personalities, but by a totally impersonal superior force called the Global Market, one of the by-products of democracy and capitalism. This phenomenon is hard to describe, as I, predictably, do not dispose of enough material yet. But it is said that it is bigger than all the Shopping Malls added together, so big that it encompasses the entire Overland, and perhaps even the Underland. From what I have heard, the Global Market is a mechanism which enables everything, and I mean literally everything, including human beings, who can be bought or sold; poor ones can become rich overnight and, vice versa, rich ones can become poor (although this happens less often). It looks like some new kind of miracle centered around possessing and tokens. And if you don't have any tokens, you are down and out. Apparently it doesn't help to pray for mercy, as the Market appears to be merciless.

One more thing: I hear from Moles living in distant places that there are tunnels being built in faraway territories, such as Kazakhstan, Uzbekistan, Turkmenistan, and others, mostly ending with -stan (this ending seems to have some secret meaning). Even if they are supposed to have both democracy and bananas now, Men there are not pleased and want to leave. So they dig and dig, and try various other methods of coming here, believing (wrongly) that what awaits them is paradise. But obviously not many tunnels have reached us yet. If it were so, we moles would be the first to know.

I am ending my presentation with—I dare say—incredible information: In the meantime, somewhere in the deserts of the Middle East—as well as in the Never-Never Land called America—huge walls were built at their borders. But it is simply hard to believe that, after the Berlin Wall, Humans would repeat the same mistake again. If so, the only thing we Moles can conclude is that there is no help for them, because they really are their own worst enemies.

VI

FROM GULAG TO GOULASH:
THE INTRODUCTION TO
MS. PIGGY'S HUNGARIAN COOKBOOK

I am not a professional cook. The life of a pig is not easy, and the life of one who is an intellectual and immigrant from Hungary is even more difficult, first of all because no one ever expects a pig to be an intellectual, an immigrant—or an amateur cook, for that matter! As if a pig in connection with any of these characterizations would be a *contradictio in adjecto*. In addition, there are many intellectuals who are unsympathetically called "pigs." This is usually the case when they sink morally, not only literally, too deeply into mud. Not to mention that we pigs are called intellectuals—also contemptuously, of course!—when we aspire to something higher than our generally low status in society.

My name is Magda. I am a female pig of the illustrious and almost extinct Hungarian Mangalitza family. Here, in London, friends call me Ms. Piggy after the famous puppet from the TV series *The Muppet Show*. Allegedly I resemble her, with my curly blond hair, being nicely rounded and very opinionated. And also "hot," because that goes without saying for any female of Hungarian origin in this male-dominated world. However, she is Miss, while I insist on being addressed as Ms. That complicates my life even more, as if it weren't complicated enough already.

I have to say that, in the first place, writing this cookbook has given me the chance to go back in time. A sentimental journey into the kitchen of my mother and my grandmother—which actually was one and the same until we moved to Budapest—remembering and re-creating the smells and tastes of my childhood. I recall my grandma taking down the dried hot paprika from the rope in the storeroom, where it had been hung to dry. As she pulverized it with her mortar and pestle, I felt the sharp smell in my nostrils. I also remember the strong smell of cabbage from my mother cooking Székely goulash and the smell of *barack pálinka* brandy. Sometimes I get carried away . . . My family comes from a small village near Kecskemét, where I used to spend my summers surrounded by the *puszta* plain and plum tree orchards. In the late autumn, the main occupation in our village used to be cooking apricots to make strong *pálinka* brandy.

My parents moved to Budapest in the seventies. They simply wanted a better life for their children, and a free education was the way to bridge social differences. Back then, and until twenty years ago, Hungarians lived under a political system called socialism. Or what in the West was wrongly called Communism (because of Communist parties' leadership in Socialist countries). Why wrongly? Because Communism, in the fulfilled vision of its theoreticians Karl Marx and Friedrich Engels, is the last stage in the development of human society, a kind of "end of history," as we would say today. Socialism was only a step along the way. Fortunately or not, depending on the political beliefs one holds, this whole Socialist practice of life, together with the Communist dream, collapsed in 1989. I was twenty-seven years old.

I have to make yet another personal remark in connection with this cookbook—I ended up writing it by chance. Not only am I not a cook, but by profession I am a political scientist. However, what does my diploma mean here, in London? During these last twenty years since I left Hungary, even though I hold a degree in Scientific Socialism from Eötvös University in Budapest I was forced to do all kinds of odd jobs. At first I was a babysitter, then a nanny, and proud to become the first pig who ever got official permission to do this job. After that I worked as a salesperson in the food department of Harrods (which came in handy for my CV later on!), then as a teacher of English for Hungarian immigrants, until I finally got employed on a TV cooking show. At least this job is fun, and I get decent money and a lot to eat. To tell the truth, my PhD would not be worth much even in Hungary, as I graduated during Communist times. So many of my colleagues who taught Marxism found themselves jobless in the "brave new world"—to quote Aldous Huxley. Moreover, a whole generation of scholars, if not two, suddenly had their pasts invalidated—even if they weren't teaching Marxism, even if they had never been sympathetic to Marxism at all. Take my friend Aniko, whose specialty was American feminist literature: She has spent much of the past decade requalifying for the same university position just because her Communist-era doctorate was no longer taken seriously. Consequently, many of us left the country after 1990. It is a sad fact of life that my education is more or less worthless in both countries, but I am reconciled to it. This cookbook testifies to that.

I slowly advanced to assistant cook on the TV show *Cook and Enjoy*, now in its fifth season. The star of our program is the not yet famous Oliver Marshall—please, note the nice twist in his name! I am one of the very few creatures who has a real insight into his cooking and who knows that he will never become as famous as Jamie Oliver! Among other tasks, I have often had to sample the food he cooks; this is what we pigs do best. And this is how this book came about. I often told Oliver: Listen Ollie (we call him Ollie because, for obvious reasons, he hates to be called Oliver), you could add a bit more pepper to that stew, or, listen Ollie, I would cut the onions more finely, because they need to actually melt . . . and so on. I have a lot of ideas of my own. One day he said, "Well, Ms. Piggy, since you are so smart, why don't you cook all by yourself, eh?"

He did not mean it seriously; his intention was to be ironical. But the producer of our show heard him and immediately thought that this, indeed, was an interesting idea. A pig who cooks? Better still, a pig writing a cookbook! Let's say, a Hungarian cookbook—because I am from *there*, am I not? "What do you think about that?" the producer asked me. "And then, perhaps, I could get you your own TV show," she added. I am not crazy about having my own show; it is a lot of work and a big responsibility for a single pig—even for a proud Mangalitza. I remember how the audience used to laugh at poor Miss Piggy on *The Muppet Show*, thinking that she was vain and stupid.

But I accepted the offer: Who, in my position, wouldn't? Considering that I can certainly cook better than Ollie, and I can write, too. Besides, there is a direct connection between cooking and politics: As a political scientist, I would argue that politics is—cooking.

There are many cookbooks in this world, too many. Sometimes, when I enter a bookstore and stop in front of shelves of them, I fall into a deep depression just looking at all that glitz and glamour.

Many cookbooks include sumptuous photos of meals; they make your mouth water. On the other hand, they look more like picture books for children than cooking manuals. I am against cookbooks with photos! For one, they make the book more expensive. Besides, they make the reader look stupid, as if he (or, more often, she!) needs to see the food in order to trust the recipe. And then, when the reader, following the recipe, makes the same meal, it looks very different on the plate. The meat is not as pink as in the photo, the bread crust is not as crispy, the salad not as green. Even the expensive tablecloth doesn't look half as good as in the photo!

Yes, I must admit that glamour, glitz, snobbery, and expensive ingredients put me off. There are, of course, many reasons *not* to write a simple cookbook, as one is inevitably discouraged to do so every step of the way. But, by the same token, this is precisely the reason for me to write a simple cookbook of my own. You have to have a passion for food (which we pigs usually have!), some basic idea of what it's all about, and a clear concept of what you want to put on the plate. And in this case that is traditional Hungarian cuisine.

My book is an antisnobbish book with simple, tasty, and easily available ingredients that you don't have to hunt for in foreign countries, I guarantee you. In my cookbook you will find recipes I cooked and tasted myself, recipes I learned from my mother back in Budapest. She had a box full of them, written down by my grandmother in her neat hoofwriting in green ink on small pieces of cardboard the size of a postcard. My grandma believed that these cardboards were more practical than a notebook or a book, because it is easier to handle a cardboard than turn a page, with an often greasy hoof. Now I have the same box in front of me. But unlike Grandma, I happen to think that a box is really an awkward way to keep recipes. Especially when you are getting ready to leave the country and have to stuff all your possessions into one single suitcase—which is exactly what happened to me in 1989. My cookbook, which you are holding in your hand or hoof right now, is a book of the same size as Grandma's cardboards, hardcover and no photos, except, of course, for the goulash on the cover.

Goulash, or *gulyás*, is a typical and surely the most famous Hungarian dish. It roughly translates as beef stew, although it is really a special kind of stew, as you will surely realize. It was invented by herdsmen (*gulyás*) from the *puszta* pastures and became extremely popular throughout the world at the beginning of the last century. In my view, its ingredients can vary as long as you throw vegetable oil (instead of the customary lard), add beef cut in cubes, onions, potatoes, garlic, and a lot of peppers into the pot and let it simmer. Tomatoes, carrots, and other vegetables are optional, although there are other, more radical opinions that exclude tomatoes altogether. But all agree about a lot of peppers. Adding more water, or less, determines if it will be a goulash stew *pörkölt* or a goulash soup (*gulyásleves*).

Before I tell you more about this cookbook, let me focus for a moment on the political aspect of goulash—that is, on the Hungarian political stew called goulash communism. After all, I was a professor of political science, and it is of the utmost importance to me to clarify the difference between two very similar words: goulash and gulag. Don't be puzzled because I mention the gulag in connection with goulash. Both have to do with socialism, and I can't hide either my past or the time when my homeland was a Socialist republic and part of the Soviet bloc. That also goes for the Soviet kind of repression. As Hungary and the USSR were not only neighbors but also, so to speak, comrades in Communism for almost five decades, it is only logical that I should feel that there is a certain danger of confusing the two words.

It is not just because they sound similar and could confuse ears not accustomed to such nuances. No, the distinction is even more important because today's reader might not be aware that gulag, as opposed to goulash, has nothing to do with food at all! Also, when you think about it, these two words are among the very few words from our part of the world that have succeeded. But the fact that someone might confuse them is not only bothersome, it is offensive to me. Because one stands for something good and the other for something horrible.

GULAG is in fact an acronym for the administration of what officially was called "corrective labor camps" in the USSR between the thirties and midfifties of the last century. Incidentally, it seems that in the USSR and other Socialist states, party and state apparatchiks loved acronyms, like RSDLP(b), CPSU, CPC, KMT, NKVD, GOELRO—our own AVH, SWP, NEM plan, and so on.

But they often hid a terrible reality—as in the case of gulags. In these camps, mostly situated in the frozen tundra of Siberia, inmates died like flies because, looking at it from my perspective, there was no goulash to eat there. Or hardly anything else, for that matter! Indeed, in a very general way, and only for the purpose of this cookbook, the gulag could be defined as a place characterized by its scarcity of food. Inmates, fed on the meager rations of *kasha* (a kind of porridge), ate rats and dogs and God knows what else—they even killed each other for a portion of food. Many of them ended up in camps for committing ridiculous "crimes" like petty theft, telling what were considered antigovernment jokes, or holding political views revealed to be "counterrevolutionary." A very wide definition of "enemy," based on the principle "he who is not for us is against us," was used to sentence them to the gulag. Innocent people were forced to live together with real criminals and murderers. Perhaps even twenty million passed through these camps, and millions perished. With the passage of time, the acronym GULAG became gulas; that is, a noun symbolizing the repressive Soviet system itself. With this transformation it also became a dangerous word. Those who knew about it had to pretend that they didn't.

I remember very well the first time I heard the word. It was in the eighties, when I read the novel *One Day in the Life of Ivan Denisovich*, by the dissident Soviet writer Aleksandr Solzhenitsyn, who himself had been an inmate for eight years. His novel tells about just that, a day in a camp, how these inmates lived in dirt, were eaten by lice, dressed in rags, and fought for the little food there was. The meaninglessness of that life seemed the hardest thing to put up with. Therefore, at the end of a day Ivan Denisovich was pleased, because he had worked hard and well. This was the first book I had read that described the gulag system and how it was used as an instrument of mental repression.

Later on, I read more of Solzhenitsyn, whose book *The Gulag Archipelago* made the gulags known throughout the world. I read Varam Shalamov's memoir *Kolyma Tales*, as well as Eugenia Ginsburg's *Journey into the Whirlwind*, and then *Within the Whirlwind*, and many more. My generation of pigs at Eötvös University was fascinated by these accounts. But one book of memoirs stuck with me, perhaps because I discovered that my father kept it hidden in his desk. It was Karlo Stajner's *Seven Thousand Days in Siberia*. Sentenced for his "antirevolutionary activities," Karlo Stajner spent twenty years of his life in camps. In his introduction to the English edition, the well-known then Yugoslav writer Danilo Kiš describes a meeting with Stajner and his wife, Sonja, who had waited for him to come back for all those years and to whom he later dedicated his memoir. In one single but tremendously powerful sentence, Kiš describes Sonja's eyes: "[T]hey are not like the eyes of the blind, not blind eyes, but eyes that no writer has ever described and few people have seen, dead eyes in a living face." Stajner was a victim—but so was she; this sentence made me never forget what the gulag had done to Sonja's eyes.

If the gulag stands for the Soviet kind of repression, in Hungary during the late sixties a set of economic changes turned the totalitarian system in another direction, toward goulash communism.

It is hard to understand any of these changes without mentioning Stalin—even if a history book, rather than a cookbook, offers perhaps a more appropriate place to learn about Joseph Vissarionovich Dzhugashvili. By removing everyone who stood in his way to ultimate power in the early thirties, he rose to the position of a Communist dictator whose nom de plume, Stalin, was given to this specific type of Socialist government—not only in the USSR. But to simplify the explanation, the reader should imagine Stalin as a kind of Darth Vader, the lord of the "dark force." On the other hand, his army did defeat Hitler. The experience of living under socialism teaches us that political leaders are neither heroes nor villains—but sometimes even both. And to go back to the *Star Wars* movie metaphor I just used, Luke Skywalker came very late to the USSR, only in the late eighties. He appeared under the name Mikhail Gorbachev, and he was not a hero from the start either, just a party bureaucrat, but that is another story.

The so-called goulash communism started when János Kádar, the general secretary of the Hungarian Socialist Worker's Party—who remained in office for more than thirty years—introduced his New Economic Mechanism, or NEM, in 1968. Not that he was such a good guy—he himself had skeletons in his closet; for instance, mass arrests right after the revolution in 1956. First students rebelled against the Stalinist type of government. When the police shot at them, the uprising spread throughout the country, and the government fell. But then the Soviets decided to step in, and the Soviet army invaded the country on November fourth. The revolution, which lasted only a few weeks, was crushed at the price of thousands upon thousands of civilians killed. A new, pro-Soviet government was installed, with János Kádar as prime minister. As Americans would say: There is no such thing as a free lunch! So Kádar ordered (or, better said, was ordered to order) the persecution of some 26,000 rebels, of whom 13,000 were imprisoned and several hundred even executed. Some 200,000 people fled the country.

On the other hand, he knew that the whole of Soviet-style socialism was hated, and he needed to introduce compromises in order to keep socialism going. And Hungarians knew that Kádar knew, and he knew that they knew that he knew.

When he introduced the new economic plan, Kádar was confronted with the same question of ingredients: How far could one go in introducing various additions and changes—and still call it socialism? His unorthodox mixture of ingredients from both the planned and the market economies made our bellies full, our newspapers more liberal, our piggish rights more respected. Our life improved. Obviously, he decided that it was better to offer a meager goulash—with somewhat unconventional ingredients—than the gulag. The main principle of goulash communism became, to quote him: "He who is not against us is for us." Instead of weeding out "counterrevolutionary" elements, Kádar sort of dumped them into his stew, which only made it thicker. It worked in the same way as when a cook adds some flour to the sauce: "With us" functioned just like that, like a cohesive element in the society, a glue of sorts. Out came a bearable, edible stew based on compromise—a golden cage of a sort.

Thus, two similar words canceled each other out: There was no goulash in the gulag—and there was no gulag in goulash communism. The reader must admit that there is a remarkable difference between these principles, marking the distinction between life and death. In a Socialist country, generally speaking, life boiled down to politics; we did not exist outside of the political realm. A wrong word and one was demoted, lost a job, or was gone forever. I happen to know this not only because I read about it, but also because this was why my cousin had grown up without a father. He was executed in the Stalinist purges in Hungary in 1949. Yes, the Communist revolution did eat its children, after all. We pigs could bear witness to that . . .

If you ask me, the era of Kádar started in 1970, when my family first bought a car, a Trabant made in the GDR. It was small and ridiculous from today's point of view, but it took us to Grandma's village, to Lake Balaton to swim—which we pigs particularly liked—and as far as the Adriatic coast of what was then Yugoslavia. At the border, though, we did encounter some minor problems, as Yugoslavs did not expect pigs to be driving a car or to have passports. Thanks to father's knowledge of their pig language, and even more to the American cigarettes he had obtained illegally, we always crossed over. Swimming in the Adriatic Sea, at the coastal town of Baška Voda, was simply a fantastic experience for us piglets. The sea was warm, blue, and transparent, and I remember seeing a tiny fish swimming close to me. Ah, those were good times for pigs! But it doesn't mean that my generation grew up politically unaware of the kind of political circumstances we lived under, especially as it was not easy to cross the border toward Italy or Austria.

By the way, let me tell you that I was among the first Hungarian pigs who, together with citizens of the GDR, crossed that very border, near Sopron, where in August of 1989 Austrians and Hungarians together cut down the barbed wire and let us cross over to the western side. How euphoric we were then . . . We believed that everything would change overnight. In fact, instead of goulash communism, we got goulash capitalism. That is, capitalism with a lot of leftovers from *Kádarism*, if one may say so. However, there is hope! Because, to paraphrase Heraclitus, one could not step twice in the same goulash. But I did not get too far. I came back home soon afterward. However, since with my qualifications I couldn't get a suitable job, I went farther west. Twenty years later, here I am in London, writing about goulash and, inevitably, about goulash communism.

Allow me, please, one more explanation: Besides writing a Hungarian cookbook, I also want to draw the reader's attention to another, if not political then important social aspect of cooking: to the fact that women usually cook for a family, and they cook every day. Even though many women would probably prefer to do it only from time to time, like men. That they have to feed us on a daily basis doesn't mean that women are not good, solid cooks and even excellent chefs. But, in contrast to men, they don't consider their daily meals as masterpieces that deserve to be admired.

Male cooks primarily want to show off. Did you ever notice that almost all great chefs are men? Why? Because males of all kinds need spectators. To them, preparing a fine meal is yet another way of demonstrating their egos. Therefore, they cook for special guests, while females do the everyday cooking. However, I have noticed that there is hope for men and other males, because a change is taking place among youngsters. You just can't overlook the fact that female and male roles in the kitchen are rapidly changing.

I think that cookbooks *should* be divided into male and female. Call me a *feminist pig* if you want, but my cookbook is a feminist one! Does that sound contradictory? The reader must wonder what a feminist cookbook really means? Does it have something to do with frozen food from a supermarket, since feminists certainly are not into spending their lives in the kitchen, as women did for generations? No, it has to do with simplicity. By the way, let me declare here and now that I consider all females of all kinds to be emancipated if they can earn their own living and can make their own decisions independently. To me, economic independence is the main criterion for emancipation.

Although feminism might sound a bit old-fashioned nowadays, it is still needed. Look at the countries in transition, where I come from. In my political scientist's opinion, women are the biggest losers with the downfall of Communism in Eastern Europe. I saw with my very own eyes how dissidents, suddenly coming to power, forgot all about their female partners. What about all the female legwork done for the "velvet revolution" to happen (although it wasn't velvet all over Eastern Europe)— from planning, discussing, writing, printing, distributing leaflets, and marching together to cooking for them, getting them back on their feet when they drank too much, or hiding them from the police? After 1990 these dissident females vanished into thin air! So much for equality . . . Obviously, there is no equality when it comes to acquiring power. Women in the former Communist countries are, generally, worse off. They were the first ones to lose jobs and the last ones to get them. A friend back home told me that her thirty-year-old daughter had to sign a secret contract when she finally got a job. She had to promise that she wouldn't have children for the next five years! And many of her friends, young females, are forced to do the same, because this is the only way to get employment. They have to live with the laws of "cowboy capitalism," more cruel than here in the West. I saw that in my part of the world there is nobody to protect women; no government will take care of their rights if they don't learn to do so themselves.

Now, my task in this book is, as I said, to introduce the reader to traditional Hungarian cuisine. Please bear in mind that I consider myself to be a patriot when I say that, compared to French or Chinese cuisine, I think Hungarian cuisine is hardly a great cuisine at all! But this goes for most other cuisines as well. In Hungarian cuisine there are a number of recipes, some of them originating in the vast plains situated between Austria to the west and Ukraine and Romania to the east—that is to-day's Hungary. But we must admit that many of these meals are just local variations of Turkish recipes. This is the case in all European countries where the Ottomans ruled for hundreds of years, places like Greece, Bulgaria, the former Yugoslavia, Romania, and, yes, my beloved Hungary.

But Hungarians believe that the world, especially real gourmets, surely knows about its fantastic achievements. As every Hungarian cookbook will proudly inform you, it has a "long and rich tradition." Of course, like all intellectuals, I like to challenge prejudices, here, for example, the notion that its tradition is *long*. Since Magyars are of nomadic origin, regardless of whether you support the Finno-Ugric, or even the most exotic Sumerian theory of their origin, it hardly facilitates cooking. It is not easy to imagine all those Magyar warriors furiously spurring their horses in order to scare off their enemies while the pots and pans tied to them (to their waists, perhaps?) are clanging and making a hellish noise. Or perhaps it was the very noise that helped them to chase away their enemies? I even dare say that this is a new and original hypothesis that might be worthwhile pursuing further!

The most characteristic spice that earned Hungarian cuisine (as well as its females!) the reputation of being *hot* is red paprika—or peppers. And although the Turks had already introduced it in the sixteenth century, it only became widely used relatively recently. We could date the traditional (i.e., hot) Hungarian cuisine back only to the nineteenth century. As for Hungarian cuisine being rich—well, let me tell you that the basic ingredients usually include various meats and poultry, as well as fish, carrots, cabbage, sauerkraut, a lot of sour cream, red beets, beans of all kinds, and mushrooms (cooked in lard, which in the modern world is absolutely unacceptable)—and there you are. It sounds to me poor rather than rich. However, one can cook fine food with these ingredients, providing that they are fresh.

Yes, it is hard for me to be a patriot in cooking, although I am expected to be just that when writing a Hungarian cookbook— even if a pig of any other nationality would be in the same position. We Hungarians still like to believe and convince others that our cuisine—well, "our" indeed!—is one of the most famous and best in the world—at least to us! I invite you to judge for yourself, to try it out. Here you will find tasty and practical meals, a bit exotic perhaps for your palate, and therefore new and exciting. But why not? Westerners always seem to be looking for these qualities in everything, although it is not clear why. I suppose that today, more than ever, people are looking for excitement everywhere.

Finally, a word about recipes.

Recently I invited a friend to dinner and served her—guess what?—goulash. She was delighted. A few days later she called me because she wanted to make it herself, which is one of the reasons for writing this book. But she did not call me to ask for the recipe. She called to tell me that she had discovered that there are too many recipes! As she did not have a Hungarian cookbook, she went on the Internet and immediately, with a single click, found hundreds of recipes for goulash at a single address! Among others, they included goulash cooked with rice, or with ground beef or even precooked meat, not to mention Parmesan cheese, ketchup, and even apples, which some people apparently add to the dish. These recipes, however, have little to do with goulash the way we Hungarians make it, or with the recipe you can find in this cookbook. In her confusion, my friend phoned me. "What shall I do?" she asked. "Is there no original, meaning one single, recipe for goulash?" She may have thought that this was a simple question, not being aware that this meal had also become a metaphor for our society—indeed, for the Socialist political regime we had. In the last decade, however, sooner than you could say the name of this stew, the recipe for goulash turned into a question of nothing less than—national identity!

The question of whether there is one original, traditional recipe (with obligatory ingredients excluding all others) for a goulash seems to be central to this discussion. But for Hungarian nationalists, the concept of national identity is modeled—I am afraid—after the old-fashioned model of national emancipation of peoples living in the Austro-Hungarian monarchy. In those days, national identity was perceived as static, as something cast in stone: There is a people; there is a language, culture, tradition—as well as a food, I might add—so there should be a state, too. And all that (except for the state) is God given and has to be guarded with one's life, because it is always under threat from its enemies. Still, today apparently there are people who propagate this calcified idea of national identity. For them, goulash is part of their Magyarness and, therefore, something sacrosanct. They fear for it now; Hungary is a member of the European Union and the forces of globalization are threatening our identity more than ever. If we are not going to disappear as a nation, we have to protect it fiercely, they say. Even if it is a question of using a tomato when making goulash! There are particularly nationalist political parties that pride themselves on being at the front line of defending this beef stew.

They promise to return its national pride and dignity, forgetting that nowadays the original ingredients mostly come from elsewhere: peppers from Holland; beef from Denmark; potatoes maybe from Spain; and garlic from as far away as China. Forgetting also that it is not in the nature of this meal to be strictly controlled, or it could easily turn into something opposite that smacks of . . . well, yes, of the gulag.

Social scientists today know that there is, of course, a modern approach to the national identity issue. From this point of view any national identity, rather than something God given is a social construct. It means something created (perhaps like goulash) as opposed to something God given (like paprika). Paprika is—well, paprika. But goulash changes constantly—as does national identity, composed of many more elements than a nationality, a language, a history, or a tradition. To such an extent that it is nowadays called a multiple identity. In the context of this cookbook, I myself would name it a sandwich identity! For example, I am of Hungarian origin, but I have dual citizenship, and my loyalties are never in conflict except during the World Cup in soccer, when I tend to root for the Hungarian team. My individual identity, my family identity as a Mangalitza pig—followed by my local, regional, national, and European identities—are not in conflict. Rather than only through national belonging (and national food), I define myself through my other interests—like my feminism, club membership, love of travel and swimming, and so on.

Therefore, in regard to the goulash-as-national-identity question, I think that it is important to stick to the basic recipe, but various additions are allowed, although (again!) the question can be raised: How far can one go and still be able to call it a goulash? But according to my friend, to my astonishment and amusement, this dilemma has already been solved on the Internet. There every mixture remotely similar to our kind of goulash is a goulash nevertheless. At least the name remains, and I hope that it is never going to be confused with gulag. Isn't that something to be proud of?

As any reader of this introduction will surely understand by now, the most important ingredient of any goulash—as well as goulash communism—is tolerance. Even though this particular ingredient is never mentioned in any Hungarian cookbook. And this is why my cookbook, in the end, is inevitably political. This is why it stands for the freedom to interpret basic recipes while still preserving the identity, the Magyarness, of the dishes, of Tokay wine, of PIK salami, and all what we call Hungarica.

I like to think of my cookbook as promoting a Hungarian nouvelle cuisine of a sort. I also like to think—perhaps this reveals my vanity!—that understanding the difference between a goulash and a gulag could contribute to understanding why it is so hard, and why it takes such a long time, to change the mentality of people who for decades were haunted by this difference.

At the end, dear patient reader, I am aware that I started this long but necessary introduction in a light tone and ended up embroiled in politics, history, and identity—just like a typical East European intellectual—and I don't apologize for that.

As for the recipes that follow, I can only wish you enjoy them regardless of how original they are! *Jó étvádyat!*

VII

AN INTERVIEW WITH
THE OLDEST DOG IN BUCHAREST

S o, my dear friend, you've come all the way from Vienna to ask why there are so many dogs on the streets of Bucharest, even in the very center? You tell me that "there are an estimated three hundred thousand stray dogs in Bucharest, a city of more than two million people, and there are up to fifty incidents of biting per day"—figures you found in the news.

Striking statistics, and true, indeed.

Forgive me for saying so, but you must be a foreigner who is here for the first time to ask about dogs. I wouldn't say that you're naive, just that this is what foreign visitors like you notice first: the impossible traffic situation and the stray dogs. At this time of day I bet it took you two hours to get from the airport to my home, although it shouldn't have taken more than thirty minutes? Am I right? Of course, but Romanians are used to it. They prefer to drive their cars, even if they have to drive at the pace of a snail. Our local humans don't notice us dogs any longer—and if they do, unlike you they seem not to consider us a problem. You see, one gets used to everything with time, even thousands of dogs in the streets of, shall we say, one of the European Union's capitals.

I agree when you say that we *cani* are cohabitants with humans as long as we don't bite them. I also agree when you say that one doesn't see thousands of dogs roaming the streets of, say, Berlin, Paris, or, God forbid, Vienna. By the way, I hear that Vienna is a kind of paradise for dogs. Not only are its citizens not bothered by dog—forgive my expression—droppings being spread all over the pavements of that beautiful city, but ladies take them along to fine coffeehouses, and waiters bring them water. Moreover, dogs are seen sitting in ladies' laps and eating cakes from small plates of their own—if one can believe *that* kind of rumor. But you're nodding! You've seen it yourself? Oh, it warms my heart that such a place exists in this cruel world! However, not even there do packs of dogs roam free.

I want to say that I understand your curiosity about this subject, my dear friend. It seems that canine freedom to move in this city somehow indicates primitivism in the local humans. Seriously, though, my opinion is that the dog question does not have a simple answer. Maybe I'm too old; maybe you should ask another dog. We dogs are just like you: Some of us don't remember; some simply don't care; and, most certainly, we have different opinions among ourselves. You happen to be interviewing a very old dog (that is me, Karl, called Charlie) who remembers that the beginning of the whole dog story in Bucharest started during the ancien régime, and who happens to think that the displacement of dogs was the consequence of a political decision. In former times, what you habitually call Communism (although there was communism and Communism), politics used to rule our lives in a more obvious way. I mean, both our and our human cohabitants' lives, since our destinies are intertwined.

Without wanting to be pathetic, I could say that we dogs were also victims of the totalitarian regime. I'll tell you how.

But I am running ahead of myself. I am prone to digressions, you know. It's my age. On the other hand, I was recommended to you precisely because of my age or, rather, for my memory, eh? How old am I, you ask? I was born during historic times, in 1990, just before the "revolution," which makes me extremely old in dog years. Or roughly 120 in human years. No wonder my mind wanders sometimes . . .

Where was I? Oh yes, that we dogs in Romania were victims of Communism. I am afraid that we are no less victims of the postrevolutionary period as well—as you can witness yourself today. My people—or should I say my kind, for the sake of what is nowadays called political correctness?—tell me that life on the streets is getting bloody tough. As if I don't see that myself, just because I don't go out for long walks anymore. Ah, my rheumatic legs! But I see, believe you me. Just yesterday I accompanied my friend (you understand, I can't call him "master")—Martin is his name—to the nearby grocery. Mind you, not one of these fancy chains sporting Dutch tomatoes that don't smell or taste of anything, like Billa or Spar, that we have everywhere now. It's a small state-owned *Alimentari* that hasn't changed for some reason. Yet. It is selling locally grown cabbage heads and half-rotten onions. And there she was, lying in front of the store, an example of our misery for all to see: a beautiful Labrador bitch waiting for someone to take pity on her and give her a piece of bread. Waiting, I say, not begging, because you could tell that she was too fine to lower herself to that level. She had sad velvet eyes that reminded me of my mother's . . . Anyway, there was another dog on a leash, tied to a fence. Although just an ugly creature of a mix breed (and I'm not being racist here, merely expressing my indignation), he looked down upon the Labrador bitch as if proud of the status indicated by the presence of his leash. A dog on a leash is in possession of something very precious nowadays: a master. For any dog in Bucharest this is no small matter, since it means he's fed regularly, which most can't claim. So he looked at the bitch, at her hungry expression, at the infected wound on her ear, and at her dirty golden coat, and I saw his look. It was full not of empathy but of malice. I was disgusted at his behavior. "Wait here," I told her, and she looked at me with gratitude. Of course my friend Martin gave her a few morsels; he's that kind of person. But that's not a solution for stray dogs; charity never is a solution for social problems.

You see, there we are, I'm calling for a systematic solution, and that, of course, is to slip into politics! Yes, politics about dogs. They, too, are intelligent creatures; they need rules.

You tell me that you recently visited New English College and that you met a dog there who was mildly curious and decidedly not aggressive. I know him; he was adopted there, lucky sod! But at least he was pleasant. There are many cases of self-adoption or semiadoption. That's when people feed the dogs in their neighborhood and in that way domesticate them. As you can imagine, one must adapt or perish. Just think, dogs were the very first animals to be domesticated by humans thousands of years ago. Isn't it a paradox that today humans are doing the same again? However, this isn't the solution either, because, as you know, my lot tends to multiply rather quickly, which is an issue I'll take up a bit later. Suddenly there are too many dogs on the streets, and nobody can feed them. And then, as a result, we become hungry—and angry. In other words, by behaving carelessly we make our own lives more difficult.

Do you see how this issue is getting more and more complicated?

You've most certainly met the kind of dog who passes you by, looking indifferent or very busy, although I can't think with what. You know, the kind who deliberately avoids even eye contact with you humans. Those wretched creatures are making an effort to maintain their pride, even if—regrettably—they know they live off humans and always have done. Nowadays, I'm sorry to say, most dogs you meet in the streets of Bucharest bark at you, and even try to bite you. As I already told you, the statistics you quoted at the beginning are true. What was that? One of your friends here had such an experience? She told you that one afternoon she was walking home in her rather posh part of town when all of a sudden a dog jumped out from under a car and bit her on the leg? And that she considers herself lucky that it wasn't a big dog, and that the wound wasn't serious. Hmm . . . your friend was indeed fortunate that a solitary dog attacked her, I'd say. Stray dogs usually operate in packs. Your friend was surely aware of that, and therefore did nothing about it, didn't report the incident to, say, the police. What would police have done? Probably just have laughed at her and told her that they are sometimes attacked themselves. Even today Romanians rarely report such incidents to the police—or any incidents, for that matter. Who trusts the police?

I'm aware that such attacks—such stray dogs—would raise alarm in any other city. A mayor would have to come up with some solution. Not here, not in Bucharest. Not even if children are attacked, which happens more than you might believe. Let me just tell you that besides organized crime and corruption, organized dog attacks are next! Alright, alright, dogs perhaps represent a different kind of danger, but again, it all depends on how you look at it.

You now ask me, How come the same people who got rid of a dictator like Nicolai Ceausescu seem not to be able to deal with dogs? A legitimate question, indeed, and one that I expected. What didn't occur to you is that perhaps people here don't *want* to deal with dogs. In a way, you see, this whole thing is Ceausescu's legacy, one of many, I might add. How did it all happen? How did he, of all people, let dogs free? Because, as you say, to imagine that he would let anyone free, even dogs, is quite difficult.

See, the street dogs of today are the great-great-grandchildren of the dogs set free in the mideighties, when the old part of central Bucharest was erased from the face of the earth. This is how it all began. And you must be wondering, on the other hand, why a totalitarian regime capable of such destruction, of uprooting tens of thousands of humans, couldn't have taken radical care of dogs? I suggest that you think about something else, about people who obediently abandoned these noble creatures, their best friends (because we're talking here about house pets) to life on the street, to the cruel struggle of survival. Doesn't that tell you something about those who didn't have the courage to defend their own homes?

Ah, blessed times, when you could blame Ceausescu for everything, I say in retrospect. At least we dogs weren't responsible for our situation.

You can tell that I'm still bitter about the whole thing. Why? Because of my mother. Mimi was a great lady. We are black poodles, with a fine pedigree. However, after that event it was unimportant who was who; class differences were forsaken because street life imposed another kind of hierarchy. The strongest, not the cleverest, ruled the rest. *Homo homini lupus*, you say to describe such a situation. But I would rather say: *canus cani homo*!

I hadn't been born when the big eviction happened—it's called resettlement nowadays. But my mother was, and she told me about it. I had the great fortune of living with her in the same household at a tender age (until Martin came along and picked me up) and so I learned my history, which today, regrettably, has been forgotten among my lot—as well yours, I'd say. These young idiots think that it's always been this way, that dogs are born and die in the streets and not, say, in a sixth-floor apartment. They'd have a heart attack if they went in an elevator. Funny, when you think about it; I've lived almost all my life in such a place. And imagine them, if you can, in the back of the car going for an excursion at the seaside! Not that many Romanians have a car, but some do. No, these poor souls think that cars are there so that they can hide from people and rain.

Simple technology such as radios or TVs are unknown to them. I'd like to know what they'd think of an airplane. I flew in one once; those were the days! I still can recall the taste of a biscuit my companion got with a cup of tea and gave to me, naturally. There's something about flying ten thousand meters above the earth looking through a window at white clouds and chewing a biscuit.

Sorry, I got carried away again.

At that time, before everything went to the dogs, as they say, we dogs were still mostly living with humans, as is the case in every normal country. In their homes and gardens, even in apartment buildings in tiny apartments. Not all of us were in equal situations, because, to paraphrase George Orwell, a writer whom I admire, "we are all equal, but some are more equal." But all of us had a minimum, a roof over our heads and a piece of bread, a bite of . . . well, at least *mamaliga*, a kind of polenta, you know. In my long life I've learned that security is what matters most, both to dogs and to humans. One can witness that now, in this period of total insecurity.

And let me tell you something else—and I'm aware that I run the risk of being judged as pro-Communist, which is foolish—we all worked! It might sound strange with all these unemployed youths on the streets to whom "work" has no meaning. What do they do? Do they hunt? Do they guard homes and defend them from burglars? Do they announce visitors? Are they employed by the police to chase criminals and sniff out smuggled drugs? Do they perhaps lead blind people through the streets of Bucharest? Or do they provide love and comfort to their cohabitants? Comparatively very few do that today. No, they live in gangs, catch rats, eat rubbish, bite children, and beg. Some end up in laboratories as well. The good news for us is that there aren't many scientific experiments going on today in Romania!

Let me go back to Mimi. My mother didn't only witness the eviction from the old quarters, but she herself, together with thousands upon thousands, was a victim of that madness. The orders to destroy the old quarters of downtown Bucharest, like the Uranus neighborhood where she had lived, came from the court, from Ceausescu himself, as did all orders. Although one could never be sure how much Elena had to do with that grandiose, maniacal plan to build a palace pyramid called (and I can't help being ironic here) the House of the People. They were both incredibly vain persons and not very intelligent. Perhaps because of that they believed they were omnipotent. Tens of thousands of people were evacuated from some eight thousand old buildings and villas into newly built apartments, gray blocks that you can still see standing today. And they were forbidden to take us along. Just when they needed us most to comfort them for their loss, as Mimi used to lament. You see, she was sad for people, not for her own destiny. That was the kind of person she was. Mimi saw with her own eyes a bulldozer destroying her beloved family home, with its yellow facade and a small garden behind. It was a horrifying scene, a huge metal hand reaching into the house and pulling out debris, like gutting a fish. Even today it's hard for me to recall how she described her feeling of helplessness as she watched the destruction. It caused her physical pain to see that, she said. Imagine it: The whole neighborhood, humans and dogs, standing there and watching, desperate, frightened, and powerless . . . without a single voice of protest.

Soon the old houses were gone, even the old scents. Now it smelled of newly dug soil, of cement and bitumen and dogs' piss. It was dangerous to go to the building site, but they all went there at first. In disbelief, perhaps, as if expecting to wake up from a nightmare. Many dogs died of hunger right away. Without food, vaccinations, and care, they were decimated quickly. They also died from depression, especially the older dogs. Mimi was young and beautiful, and a woman from the outskirts of Bucharest took pity on her. So, I was not born in the street. She always reminded me how privileged we were.

Anyway, my mother was well connected and had a relative who lived close to the court. He told her that the Ceausescus had two pet dogs. This might surprise you, because you know that both Nicolai and Elena came from a village and that peasants have only working animals, not pets. Besides, Nicolai would never have petted a dog because of his mad fear of bacteria that made him change into a new suit every day. This was a kind of posing, though. Tito of Yugoslavia had two white poodles, not to mention the American president, the Queen of England, and other "decadent" characters. If it took pet dogs to be considered posh—so be it! Nicolai had a huge black one called Corbu (the Raven) who, they say, had the military rank of colonel and was driven around in an official car. And our queen, she had a lovely cocker spaniel, whose name escapes me now.

No, no, I'm not exaggerating! I know for sure because once, a very long time ago, our cousin Nicu was taking care of some children on vacation in a little house in the mountains close to the Ceausescus' villa. One beautiful sunny winter's day the children were out playing in the snow when all of a sudden he didn't hear them anymore. There was a total silence. Nicu looked through the window and they were lying on their backs perfectly still, with a huge black dog standing over them. He rushed out and saw the two Ceausescus walking with the cocker spaniel at their heels. A Securitate officer, very elegant in his military uniform, was trailing behind them. Nicu happens to be a Doberman, so he started walking toward Corbu with a murderous look in his eyes. Just then the officer called the dog back. Apparently Corbu was trained to pull down to the ground and hover over anything that moved when the couple was around. Even while telling this story, our brave cousin would shake with rage. So yes, the Ceausescus were snobbish about the breed of their dogs and "walked them" now and then.

Nicu, who obviously belonged to a *nomenclatura* family close to the court, also swore he'd witnessed an interesting scene years later. He was there when it was reported to the royal couple that there were too many dogs roaming free on the streets. Elena laughed. "Thousands of dogs out on the streets? Well, this is really funny," she allegedly said. "Why not kill them all?" she added, waiving her hand and dismissing the whole issue as a big joke. Her husband, meanwhile, didn't even bother to listen. I wonder what Corbu or her own dog thought about those words? I bet they were as arrogant and mean as she was. That's what you humans say about us, that we acquire the character, even the face, of a master. Although in my long life I've seen that the reverse can also happen.

Interestingly enough, and very unusually so, if I may add, Elena's remark was not taken as a command but rather as just that, a remark. Someone in the court, either very clever or very cunning, decided that people in Bucharest were shaken enough after being evicted, and that it could have been dangerous to upset them even further by exterminating dogs. It must have been an experienced courtier to realize that an additional blow like that could shift the delicate balance between the oppressed and the oppressors. The totalitarian power structure resembles a house of cards. You should be very careful when you try to remove a single card, that we all know. But, oddly enough, it's hardest to remove a card from the very top—then it's called a coup d'état. This is exactly what happened some years later, right? In other words, there was no need to demonstrate power at that particular moment. Imagine, thousands of dogs lying dead in streets, killed with rat poison, and not enough rubbish trucks and manpower to collect them: the unbearable stink, not to mention the danger of an epidemic. Plus, there were all those foreign correspondents to consider; the whole world would have known about Ceausescu's cruelty to animals. It was used to his cruelty to people. The Ceausescu regime was a murderous one, but it didn't give its enemies the pleasure of seeing it demonstrated on dogs!

So we lived on.

Well, I also happen to know the story about how dogs were saved. Yes, there is some advantage to being old, if your brain doesn't turn into pudding. It was told by a director or a manager of a rubbish removal company. Today he would be called a CEO, which is a funny title when connected with rubbish, you have to admit! One day Comrade So-and-so was called to the ministry of police (everything had to do with police in those days). Naturally, he believed that he had done something wrong. In Ceausescu's Romania one had to consider such a possibility, because the rules were decided by one person alone—Ceausescu himself—and therefore arbitrary. And how arbitrary! For example, it was notorious that Nicolai had some digestion problems. Therefore his "morning decisions," as they were called among courtiers, were—so to speak—softer than the afternoon or evening ones. It was also well-known (at least, it was an urban myth) that his cook was instructed to put a small amount of laxative into his meal if he needed to be "mollified" before an important decision had to be made. Servants actually had an important role in our history; if you only think how someone's destiny depended on Ceausescu's indigestion!

So this CEO of the rubbish removal company turns up at the ministry, his knees going weak as he enters the office of the minister. But the minister, an old pal, hugs him reassuringly. On the other hand, they would do that even before stabbing you in the back. Only after a couple of French cognacs (someone's bribe, he was sure) does our garbage man come to his senses and realize that the minister really has summoned him for a so-called consultation. Since he knows only too well that this could be a method of handing over responsibility for a problem, he's not completely relaxed, is he?

Finally, the minister asks him what it would take to clean the city streets of dogs. The rubbish removal man gives the question some quick, serious evaluation. He knows which direction the wind blows in, but that's not difficult, because it always blows from the same direction. From the minister's tone of voice he notices that "cleaning" the city of dogs is not formulated as an order (the minister could have simply said: "Kill them"), which gives him room to maneuver. "Well, it would certainly take a lot of work," the rubbish removal man says. "Plus, it wouldn't *look* nice." He's well aware that some decisions in his job are taken according to how nice or not nice the result would appear. Not inside the country, but to foreigners, to the enemies, and they are many. "There was a lot of negative publicity abroad because of the demolition of parts of the old town, so why risk more of it," he adds cautiously. "Also, there are a lot of animal lovers out there who would go berserk."

The minister looks at him without moving a muscle. "Mikhail," he says, feeling secure enough to switch to the minister's first name now, "all I'm saying is that it could be done, dogs could be exterminated. My men—with the help of the army, of course— could gather the carcasses and burn them within a week. But you should be aware that this operation is a sensitive one. All this would be very, very visible!" He sees the impact of his words on Mikhail's face, which starts to crease into a grimace that looks faintly like a smile. "Perhaps it's better to let nature take its course," our man finally concludes, thinking of food shortages for people, never mind dogs. Upon hearing that euphemism for starvation, Mikhail's face lights up. *"Let nature take its course,"* he repeats, excited, as if this banal phrase were some kind of wisdom bestowed upon him by god almighty. As he exits the office, the minister hugs the rubbish removal man once more, this time cordially. Because, you understand, the minister didn't care at all for the destiny of our canine species. He wanted the easiest way out for himself.

The CEO was right; dogs died in silence and no bad publicity was created. Anyway, much bigger political issues soon arose. Madame Ceausescu had no time to think about dogs any longer, or of anything else, for that matter. A couple of years after this incident, her time was up. Truth be said, after being abducted, an improvised show trial was organized and they both were shot like a couple of old beggars. Ceausescu went down in history as a dictator, and most people here think that they both got what they deserved. I would have wanted to see them tried, real and proper. But that wasn't to be. Romanians are foxy people; why complicate things with a trial? Why risk that the mad pair might say something unpleasant about others who had executed their orders and remained alive and kicking, as born-again "democrats"?

Soon the "let nature take its course" approach took another direction, one unpredicted by our garbage man, the minister, or anyone else. Living without any control, dogs started to multiply. In some two decades, from a mere few thousand, we grew to a few *hundred* thousand. The turbulence society was going through was called a revolution, though it would be more accurate to describe it, as I already pointed out, as a political coup. The best organized forces, such as the Securitate, the police, and the military, assumed power. Nobody cared about dogs.

It was only about a decade later, in 2001, if I remember rightly, that dogs became the center of attention. By that time we really had become visible, and a new, modern generation of Romanians who barely remembered anything about life under Communism became worried about animal rights. Imagine! Not people's rights but animals' rights! They pleaded for shelters, medicine, vaccination, and sterilization, all the right things, of course. In spite of homeless people, jobless people, hungry people on our streets, so many children begging that you could not walk freely, children who lived in a sewage system not even like dogs, but like underdogs. Frankly, as much as I was impressed by these dog lovers, I was puzzled as well. Then a certain animal benefactor, a French lady and former famous actress named Brigitte Bardot, who had allegedly been a great sex symbol in the ancient time of the sixties, responded to their pleas. And she still held power over the media. It was big news. She even visited Bucharest, met the mayor, and donated money. I still remember how newspapers reported it: "Ms. Bardot has agreed to donate more than $140,000 over two years for a mass sterilization and adoption program for the city's strays, estimated to number 300,000 . . . For his part, the mayor of Bucharest, Traian Basescu, has agreed to kill only dangerous, old, or terminally ill dogs . . . Mr. Basescu had earlier insisted that the dogs . . . must be exterminated."

Well, what can I tell you? There was no intention to "exterminate" the dogs in the first place. Afterward, that lady's money went to a few shelters, a few sterilizations—you can recognize these dogs by yellow tags they wear on one ear—and that was that. Most of it just disappeared, as usual.

Listen, I have a nice detail for your dog story. In the spring of 2008, city authorities cleared all the stray dogs out of the way so that foreign politicians coming to the NATO summit could pass undisturbed from the airports to the House of the People, where the summit was held. All the existing shelters were apparently filled with these dogs. You see, typically, our authorities only act when pressured from outside.

"It's one of these bittersweet tales," you remark. Bitter, yes, but not sweet. I remember times when Ceausescu's police would clear all "suspicious elements" of your own species from the streets; now they are down to clearing away dogs. Strange, very strange.

No doubt, this represents progress. This is the twenty-first century; we are in the European Union. Except that all Romanians ever cared about was appearance, not a solution! I'd say that Romania hasn't changed much in that respect. The "dog problem" hasn't been solved, if stray dogs ever really were a problem for the people of Bucharest, which nowadays I doubt more and more. You rightly observe that not much was done about dogs except when foreigners got involved. This, however, brings us to the beginning of this conversation. You've listened patiently to such a long monologue from an old fool and received no real explanation. But if you look around, what else can you see besides stray dogs and clogged traffic? You see, again, old, beautiful (even if decrepit) villas being demolished to make room for new buildings of steel and glass—for foreign banks and corporations, like in Shanghai or Singapore. For new masters, who no longer rule by fear but by greed.

In the transition from Communism to capitalism, all people are unequal, but some are more unequal than others.

Stray dogs don't fit into that new capitalist Bucharest, and mayor after mayor promises to do something about them. But he never acts. Probably there are many reasons for not acting and, moreover, for not knowing how to act. One could certainly blame it on cowboy capitalism, corrupt bureaucracies, bad politics, or disappointment with the EU. But I happen to believe that in Romania dogs are considered as much the victims both of Communism and the democratization process (or the transition period, as they call it) as your own kind. I observe that when an individual in this society feels pretty lost and helpless, he doesn't know how to take responsibility for his own life, much less for that of the poor dogs in his neighborhood. It doesn't help that democracy, so far, means only that those who are up stay up, like in a kind of a merry-go-round of power. It also could be a laissez-faire attitude of this society in general, which hasn't woken up properly from the Communist slumber. Generally speaking, people still believe that there will be always someone "up there" to make a decision in their names— whom they can blame later on. If yesterday it was Communism, today it is the bureaucracy in Brussels. Leaving everything to the higher-ups, not taking the initiative, not willingly acting in the common interest—this, in my modest dog's opinion, is really what our problem is. What do you do *when there's not even an idea of a common interest, a common good*? In a society like ours it needs to be created. The lack of it means that one day we'll wake up to a decision of someone high up that dogs finally have to go. In the name of the EU we'll be swept away for good. Then there will be a short outrage; the party in charge will perhaps lose a few votes. So what?, one may think. But, permit me to say these harsh words: The question is, Who will be next? Gypsies, perhaps? Jews? And why not people with glasses?

Sorry, sorry. As I said, I tend to get carried away. Look at me, an old dog giving speeches! As you can see, in Romania even dogs are political animals.

You could almost take this whole canine story as a metaphor for humans in Romania: victimized, abandoned, poor, hungry for everything, totally disillusioned. But this would be a bad metaphor, because, unlike humans, dogs won't get together and vote for someone like Napoleon (I'm referring to *Animal Farm*, George Orwell's ingenious parable) or go and start a war. And here I would like to leave you, my friend, to ponder over the frustrations that lead to populism—and to wait and see what these newly declassed masses will come up with, who will manipulate them and how.

But before we part, let me tell you just one more story. Have you heard of the "Baghdad Pups"? No? Of course not, this is a typical American venture. It's about stray dogs in Afghanistan and in Iraq and about American soldiers who befriended them. Boys wanted to take their friends back with them to the United States, but it proved to be against the law. However, a certain navy lieutenant was so in love with his dog, Cinnamon (what an idiotic name for a dog, I must say!), that he managed to do the impossible. He gave Cinnamon to a contractor, who took him to Bishkek in Kyrgyzstan. But the man could not put the dog on a civilian flight to the United States, so he abandoned Cinnamon at the airport. An airline employee gave the pup to a local family. Then the lieutenant's energetic sister stepped in and, with the help of some organization or other, located the lost dog. Now Cinnamon lives happily ever after in Maryland. Americans being Americans, they immediately realized that there are more soldiers who would like to do the same, so they organized "Operation Baghdad Pups." Their newspapers report that so far more than thirty pet formerly stray dogs have been brought over—don't ask how! The point is that Americans do things by themselves. They don't wait and despair.

Now, what shocked me are the costs of such rescue trips, between four thousand and six thousand dollars per dog. This gave me an idea. True, unfortunately Romania is not occupied by American soldiers. But why shouldn't we take action ourselves and, under the slogan "Exportation, not extermination" (I imagine this could catch media attention), offer our dogs for adoption abroad? I'm sure that there are people willing to take them; costs would be one third of the American costs, if not less. Remember how Westerners were crazy about adopting our children from orphanages? Not that dogs are as popular as white orphans, but one could at least try. For example, what if adoption included a free long weekend in Bucharest with your future pet? Of course, someone is bound to label this "dog tourism," but I think it is better and more decent than, for example, sex tourism. The more I think about the idea, the more I like it. But being an old and experienced dog, I suspect that Romanians would rather do real business by selling dogs to the Koreans as meat! In fact, I'm surprised that no one has already had that idea. The state would probably subsidize it, and some smart-ass with good connections would get rich over our dead bodies. And then he'd launch himself head-on into politics, including in his program the defense of animal rights! None of that would surprise me—especially because I heard rumors that something similar happened in the Chinatown of Budapest. But what's that you say? I see your face; you're smiling and shrugging your shoulders. You must think I'm mad.

Hey, relax. After all, I'm only a dog!

VIII

THE UNUSUAL CASE
OF THE PSYCHOTIC RAVEN

Look, I have here a notebook from my mother. She died last week, and I came to Tirana to attend her funeral. I found it among a few possessions my mother took to the hospital with her. I am now bringing her notebook to you because you are my old friend and publisher. I would like you to tell me what to do with it, if anything. Is it perhaps worthwhile publishing it—maybe not in this form, but as a contribution to a book about Communism in Albania? No, no, let me try again: What I want to say is that her notes should be published if you were to find them interesting. I don't know if this is the time to do it either—you know better than I what it means. I have been living in America for such a long time, fifteen years now, that I don't really know how things work in Albania any longer. I only remember that, when I studied here in the nineties, I often heard "it's not the time yet" for mentioning or publishing this or that. So, who am I to say?

Leafing through this handwritten notebook both out of a daughter's sentimentality and curiosity, I discovered something interesting. Apart from notes about books she had read of late, thoughts for articles she intended to write, and quite lucid observations about her own illness, I found a kind of short diary from December 1981. Well, not a diary exactly, but notes about just one very particular case she had to deal with as a psychiatrist at the Tirana Psychiatric Hospital. As you can see for yourself, this slim, older volume was carefully glued into another notebook. Not only that, it was written with a pencil rather than a pen. I imagine she did it on purpose, so that she could erase certain details in case of an emergency. I mean, it is now 2009, and yet Mother took these notes to the hospital with her. Why? What was she hiding? Of whom was she afraid, even today?

As I started to read it, I soon discovered that she had good reason not to want to part with it, even on her deathbed. In it, she describes a meeting so peculiar that at first I was not sure whether I should believe it ever really happened.

The first entry is dated December 18, 1981:

This afternoon a raven flew into my doctor's office through an open window. I was alone. My nurse had gone out on an errand, and perhaps that was the moment he had been waiting for. Nevertheless, I offered him a seat, but he preferred to stand during this first, brief, conversation. To an ordinary person he probably looked just frightened. But I immediately saw that he was in a state of a shock. He was shaking violently, could not concentrate, and had difficulty speaking—all the symptoms of severe distress were there. My first reaction was to give him an injection of a tranquilizer, which he refused. I was worried that he might experience a heart attack in such a state. He clearly was confused, disoriented, and delusional. Possibly a temporary psychosis?

After a while, he managed to tell me that he had come to ask if it would be possible to see me in private. Normally, if I had been on-call, I would have given him an injection and admitted him to our acute psychiatric ward. I would then have reported the case at our morning meeting the next day, whereupon the head of the psychiatric unit would have decided what kind of treatment he would get. If, after a few days of observation I had been put in charge of writing the report, he would have been diagnosed as not a very severe case and would have been injected with some more tranquilizers. Unfortunately, we do not have much choice in our methods of dealing with such patients. If, on the other hand, he had been diagnosed as a severely ill patient—well, then he would have been subjected to the more drastic so-called standard procedure. I happen to disagree with it, but I cannot say it so openly.

When Comrade Raven asked me to see him privately, I was taken by surprise. Who could have possibly told him about my interest in individual therapy (not to mention psychoanalysis, a word that I barely dare to write down)? Now it was my turn to get agitated: Such a visit could mean the end of my career. But I tried not to show him *how much his question had startled me. My interest in different practices within psychiatry was not really a secret, because I had written academic articles about it. However, they were only about theory—presenting the ways in which colleagues in other countries dealt with particular kinds of psychosis. That was considered daring enough. But I had gone even further, and only a couple of close friends and colleagues know that I am actually treating a few patients privately (without payment, of course). Therefore, Comrade Raven's presence in my office and his request could have meant only one of two things: that someone from our small circle of doctors had sent him to me for help—in which case I should have been informed. Or that my secret was out and Comrade Raven was here to arrest me. My "sin" was punishable in the same way as witchcraft. For a split second I had doubts as to which of the two was the case. But his state could not have been faked easily, so I decided that it really did not matter who he was, because Comrade Raven needed my immediate help.*

I calmed him down and tried to find out what had happened to him. But my usual questions made Comrade Raven still more agitated, even frightened. I saw that there was no other way to soothe him than to promise that I would see him later that evening.

Reading Mother's notes was very confusing for me. My first reaction was that this must have been some kind of mistake, or at best a joke. Why would a patient enter through the window in the first place? Was she serious when she wrote that it was a bird? Or was there something hidden behind this description? If so, how was I supposed to understand it?

Obviously she took the notes to the hospital knowing that they would come into my possession after her death, so they must have been especially important to her. But I must confess that, at the very beginning, I wondered if the notes weren't the fruit of my mother's imagination. Or if she hadn't perhaps written them already under the influence of her not yet manifested brain tumor (which was discovered much later—luckily it was one of the slow-growing kind). Or were they the result of some of the medications she had been taking for her constant migraine? After all, she could have even been hallucinating. How else could I explain to myself the fact that my mother, in her diary, described a patient as—a bird? My mother was a psychiatrist, not a veterinarian! And even if she had been a veterinarian, it seems rather strange that a raven would have had the ability to talk, although there have been cases of this very intelligent bird being able to utter a few words.

I mean, yes, she worked with all kinds of delusional patients, but she would not have written something like this in her diary—look here, she wrote *raven* without quotation marks. She would not have written that without a reason. Besides, my poor mother was not very good at pretending! For example, in the next sentence she invites the "bird" to sit down. How naive she was, if indeed her intention was to hide something. And almost right away she calls this bird "Comrade Raven"?

The other thing I found strange in this excerpt was her claim that psychoanalysis, or even individual psychotherapy, was punishable. Surely she did not mean punishable by law, because there is no reference to it in the law at all. She must have meant ideological condemnation of this Western—and therefore, by definition, negative and dangerous—practice. By the way, I happen to know that there is astonishingly little psychoanalytical practice even today. Not only in Albania but in the whole of the formerly Communist Europe as well. Obviously, the Communists did not care about individuals, much less about the problems of their psyche. I visited Mother at her workplace a few times to get an idea . . .

Now, listen to this sentence again: *"He had come to ask if it would be possible to see me in private."* This, I believe, must have been a very unlikely request at the time. First of all, the word "private" is a highly suspicious word in itself, in any context. In a Communist country where there is hardly any privacy, it is loaded with negative meaning, suggesting that a person has something to hide. Otherwise, why privacy? A stranger doesn't walk into your office, much less fly in through the window and ask to see you in private—and in a human, if agitated, voice. She rightly suspected him of being an agent provocateur sent by the secret police. My mother was a pioneer when, as early as 1993, she started psychotherapy, publicly, with individuals in her work with hospital patients. In 1981, as she writes, she started this practice in great secrecy and with only a few non-hospitalized patients. What were the risks involved in seeing patients privately at that time? There was no such thing at all as private practice in Albania in 1981. I imagine she would not only have been stripped of her license, but also imprisoned. Therefore, it was perfectly possible, if the rumor about her seeing patients outside of the hospital leaked out, for an undercover policeman to have been sent to her disguised as a sick man imagining he was a bird. I have heard of such provocations, although Mother never spoke about it.

But I also asked myself another question: Was this birdlike person perhaps someone she recognized, someone well-known, a public person, so to speak? This might have been her motivation for disguising his identity so carefully and hiding her notes about him. Perhaps, besides her professional consideration, there was another, more personal one—her fear of him? But I asked myself all these questions before finishing my reading. . . .

I realized that she must have written about this case in a coded language. Raven was his code name in the diary; she never mentions his real name, or any other particular characteristic of his looks or profession, except for his symptoms. If discovered, she could have claimed that the man required therapy and had been referred to her just because, in his severe state of acute psychosis, he identified himself with a raven.

However, the question remains—and I can see it in your eyes—why that particular bird, why *a raven*? I intuitively sensed that this name held the secret of the story, the secret of the person. I remember from my school days—as you surely do, too—that in Albanian mythology a raven is the bearer of bad news. Often it symbolizes death. It could also be a witness to something horrible. Was the name chosen as an indication she wanted to give to a future reader, to me? As if, by choosing this name for her patient she wanted to prepare me for the kind of problem she had to deal with?

Yes, I believe she was trying to warn me that what I was about to read was a dark, dangerous, perhaps mortally danger-ous, story. And yes, she wanted me to read it only after she had gone.

At first, when she suggested the nearby park as their meet-ing place, he almost went mad with fear! "The other birds might hear us," he whispered to her. Since under no conditions would Commrade Raven talk to her in the hospital, my mother agreed to see him privately. Mother writes that she had no al-ternative if she wanted to help the poor *creature* than to see him outside of the hospital. The "creature," she writes, thus adding to the ambiguity surrounding the person in question. By the way, this is another word that can have a negative connotation. The more I think about it, the more I am convinced that, in this respect, she deliberately wanted to create confusion for the possible unintended reader.

I have to tell you, I was totally amazed that my mother risked so much to write this in 1981. In my view, this must mean that the creature was someone special in her eyes—that he had a grip on her. Or that he possibly had even threatened her. The further on I read, the more concerned I became about this strange decision of hers to write about it.

Apparently, after they met that very evening, she jotted down that Raven had repeatedly said that he had seen some-thing happen in the house of the prime minister. He could not stop seeing the picture in his mind's eye. "Blood, very much blood," he told her. "That word was a trigger," Mother noted. "Whose blood did you see, Comrade Raven?" she asked him. It took her some time to understand that Comrade Raven, as she continued to call him, was highly psychotic because of the terrible event he had witnessed the previous night.

However, that same evening, during his second visit, he seemed coherent enough to tell her what had happened! Because, if she diagnosed him as highly psychotic, I suppose he could not have expressed himself in the precise sentences I found in her notebook. So, either he was psychotic and the story was constructed from bits and pieces. *Or the persona was not psychotic at all*, and this was her way of dealing with the information that he, for some reason, had confided to her. This is also a realistic option in interpreting her notes, as you will see later on. It takes a special talent to read between the lines— as we were all trained to do—but at the same time not to overdo it. When there is no information, only symbols, riddles, and guesswork—as was often the case in Albanian newspapers and books—there is a problem. One needs to decide which interpretation is the more plausible.

"It happened during the night between the seventeenth and eighteenth, in the protected zone of the Bllok," Comrade Raven said. "As it happened, I was positioned on a maple tree near the villa of the prime minister. Perched on a branch overlooking the first floor, I could clearly see his study with its dark-wood desk and old-fashioned lamp, his chair and paintings hanging on the wall. I could also see his bedroom (he sleeps separately from his wife). I

perhaps should say that, although there are curtains on that window, on the said night the curtains were not drawn.

"As I am sure you yourself noticed, there was a storm last night. It was raining heavily, strong gusts of wind bowed the trees, and dramatic bolts of lightning created a heavy atmosphere. Ominous, one might say in hindsight."

Here Mother tried to interrupt him—this word ominous bothered her and she wanted him to focus on it, on his choice of the word—but Comrade Raven indicated that he didn't want to be interrupted. See, it was already obvious to me that he didn't want to be taken on as a case, to be analyzed, that is. But Mother didn't see that yet, which surprised me. She didn't know that *he only wanted her to listen to him.*

More description follows, then Comrade Raven comes to the point:

"At first nothing happened. It was already late at night, past midnight, but the man sat there at his desk, almost motionless. After a while he stood up, looking at his watch and then through the window, as if expecting a visitor. A moment later he turned his head toward the door. He did not nod or show any sign of recognition. But I am sure that someone entered his study at this point. However, I couldn't say that for a fact. I only saw a giant shadow against the white wall in the room. Why do I even think of it as a man's shadow? I could not say if it was a

man's or a woman's; it did not have the distinct shape of a human being or any distinct shape at all, for that matter.

"It is this shadow that bothers me now . . . For the next few hours, it dominated the room of the minister, somehow looming over him, overwhelming him. No, not for a moment did I see the person who owned that shadow—if indeed there was one. I only saw something, another presence (that would be the most exact word) moving in the room, bending over the man at his desk, the light, the wall . . . Looking at the scene from outside, it appeared to me as if this shadowy presence was reproving the minister. That it was threatening him. Because the closer it came to him, the more he leaned back in his chair, until he just slumped, covering his face with his hands—as if to protect himself against an assault. It was a desperate gesture, as if he were saying, Why don't you believe me? and at the same time pleading for understanding—not for mercy, no! I don't think so, although the atmosphere appeared to me as menacing . . . And in view of what happened afterward, when the shadow . . . well . . .

"Perhaps I should have come closer to the window. But I couldn't, because of the storm.

"Then the shadow left the room, or at least moved somewhere where I could not see it any longer.

"He was a very proud, I dare say, very stiff man. I am sure he pleaded for understanding. But understanding of what? And to whom? Whose was that ominous presence in his room on that terrible night of the storm? They

*say that the Devil can be recognized by his lack of a
shadow. But I thought afterward—what is one supposed
to call a shadow without a man? Can you tell me, Comrade Doctor?"*

Well, I certainly am not willing to believe that Raven engaged in such metaphysical questions that evening with my
mother. The shadow must have had a distinct shape, you know.
It loomed and looked gigantic because of the effect of the light,
no doubt. But it was definitely a man who visited the minister, someone he knew well, since he showed no surprise. An
old friend, perhaps? My question is more down-to-earth: Why
did Raven (see, I accept the Aesopian language of my mother)
spy on the minister that night, unless this was precisely his
duty?

Anyway, my mother just listened as he went on:

*"The minister sat at his desk for a long time; I thought
he'd fallen asleep. Then he stood up and came to the window again. I clearly saw his very pale face as he pressed
his forehead against the cool glass.*

*"What happened afterward occurred in plain view.
But—how to tell you? I did and I did not see it. How can
I explain it? If it hadn't been for that shadow, whose
presence was almost more real than the minister himself,
I'd say I had witnessed a classic suicide. The minister
first took a sheet of paper and a pen and wrote a short
note—I mean, it didn't take long, the writing. Then, as if*

he had an afterthought, he reached for another sheet of paper and wrote something; this time it took longer, because he paused several times. Only then did the minister take a pistol from the drawer and put it on the desk, keeping it under the palm of his hand a while, as if warming it up. As far as I could see, he did not look desperate but rather calm. But before he pulled the trigger, I realized that he saw the shadow again! It had never left his room . . . The minister looked at it, his eyes wide open with fear, and then quickly pulled the trigger. As his head fell forward, I saw first a fountain of blood gush out, and then crimson drops slowly slide down the wall behind him . . .

"And then . . . and then . . . I saw the most incredible, most horrendous thing happen. I saw it—I did!—the shadow come up to him and lean over his body, as if checking to see that he was really dead. It then switched the light off and left the room. I swear I saw the light go off.

"When I think now that I am the last being who saw him alive . . ."

Here Mother writes in her notes that, at this point, she suggested that he might have taken some substances and suffered from a hallucination. But my impression is that she wrote this not as a real possibility but only as part of what she thought was her carefully constructed fable. In any case, he responded to her:

"Was I imagining a shadow? Hallucinating? Seeing the effect of the lamp light that night? Yes, that is of course possible. But what confuses me is that the whole thing, the duel between that wretched man and the shadow, lasted so long. Probably a couple of hours, although it seemed to me like the whole night now. Could I have really been looking at some kind of play that nature had arranged for me? Or was it a shadow-theater performance? No, I don't think so . . .

"You see, I am convinced that the shadow was . . . his soul. What is a shadow without a body? If it is not another shape assumed by the Devil, then it must be the soul. But the minister's soul was a dark, menacing, evil soul. Yet, his own! This was the most tragic thing for me, to see how dark his soul was."

I think that my mother wanted to comment on this but then gave up. There are traces left of her writing that she obviously erased. It must have been fascinating for her to hear raven (or Raven, or whoever that person was) mention both the Devil and the soul. Albania was proud of being the first atheist country in the world! No churches to pray in here; they were all turned into storehouses or assembly halls, over two thousand of them, of all denominations. It also meant that religious concepts and expressions such as the Devil and the soul were exorcised from the language. From the public language, that is. Yet it would have been highly unlikely that a person used them even privately, and in such a matter-of-fact manner, as if he really believed they existed! Well, perhaps not, if that person also was really a patient believing he was a bird, of course. But what if this person was only disguised as a patient by my mother? So he could say what he wanted, all the while being treated (in her notes) as a psychotic persona. I think that she might have herself put these religious words into Raven's mouth, just to illustrate to the outsider (the unintended reader) how sick he was, since no person in his right mind would ever utter them.

"Now, how could I tell anyone but you what I saw—a murder committed by a soul? But you agree that what I saw could indeed have been his own dark soul that pushed him into performing such an act? Metaphorically speaking, you say . . . Why did I never think of that? Of course, it is possible that he fought with himself and that his own bad conscious forced him into suicide. He had a lot on his conscience; maybe that is what killed him in the end. He was his own worst enemy; every man is. But in your interpretation that would mean the man in question had a conscience, which I am not so sure about."

This was the last she heard from Raven. He disappeared from her life as suddenly as he had entered it—however, this time not through the window. At least, she doesn't bother to mention this detail any longer. He left a doubt behind, a hint, a seed of suspicion that, after all, it might not have been a simple suicide but rather a kind of assisted suicide—even if assisted by the mysterious shadow. Although it remains unclear what Raven meant by the shadow. Or what he really saw, for that matter.

My reading of her notes is this: Comrade Raven did not pretend to be a bird, the bearer of bad news. He did not imagine or hallucinate blood. He was a person in power who saw the suicide of the prime minister that night. But the man could not keep his secret any longer and just cracked. He perhaps really lapsed into a temporary psychosis. It probably does not happen very often in his line of work, but one cannot exclude such a possibility. And he felt a strong urge to tell what he saw, to get it out, to confide in somebody. In all probability he was unlikely to talk to a friend or his wife. Whom could he turn to, I ask you, but to a professional who would keep his secret ("how could I tell anyone but you?")?

I can tell you that I was not only puzzled by the symbolism of the raven, or the question of Raven's identity, but also—as I mentioned to you earlier—by the *form* my mother had chosen to express herself. You see, from what I read and detected, and there are many other interesting details in her notes, as you will undoubtedly discover yourself, I am convinced that Raven was *not only a witness, but also the executor.*

Whoever that persona was, he was sent to the minister not only to deliver the judgment of the powers that be, but to execute it as well.

My mother, once burdened by his terrible secret, confided it to her diary—but not in simple words. She chose the form of a fable. The story of a bird—very much in the tradition of folktales. I think she was careful to compose his story in a literarily convincing way. Her fear and her conscience turned her into a writer—but isn't that often the case in many a dictatorship? Not that it helps; many writers have experienced just the opposite. Therefore, she hid it carefully.

From some of her comments (and I read you only a few) I see that she, too, suspected that Raven himself had been present in the room both before and during the suicide. Her suspicion— or, better said, her intuition—was that he was there in order to actually explain to the minister that suicide would be the only honorable way out of the impossible situation he had put himself in. Should the minister have had any doubts, that is. Maybe he did not have any doubts; yet Raven spoke about a battle of some kind. Could the two of them have been arguing? After all, according to the notes it seems that their conversation lasted quite a while.

In the end, the one who dispatched him had to be sure of the result, it seems, so the shadow persona waited until the "self-execution" (Mother uses that expression in one place) was over and checked that the minister was dead. Like a real professional. If we are to take the whole fable seriously, which she obviously did.

You will notice that she does not write further of this highly unusual "case" or of this "patient." That is strange to me (or not strange; it's indeed logical, depending upon what interpretation you prefer). Had Raven been a true patient, there would have been plenty of material to analyze and write about in scientific publications or conference papers. Why did she stop writing about him so abruptly?

Well, in a way she did not stop. She continued to write about the suicide of the minister. But from another, public side this time. Mother wrote about the real case that had actually motivated her patient—the visitor, witness, or whatever he was—to visit her:

Sure enough, during the next few days the suicide of the prime minister was in the news: The prime minister had been found dead at his home; he had killed himself as the result of a "nervous breakdown." The news report was short and scarce of details. Therefore, as usual, gossip filled the space left by the news. There were so many gossips in town; his death shook the place almost like an earthquake. Of course, the official story was that he was suspected of collaboration with the so-called enemy forces of the KGB, the CIA, UDBA, and whatnot.

The unofficial story, however, was that one of his three sons was engaged to marry a girl from a highly suspicious background: Her family had relatives in America. At first there was no obvious reaction to the news of the engagement, but then the buzz started: What was the meaning of the prime minister allowing such an act? It was not a simple act of engagement like any other. Being so highly positioned in the Communist Party and the state hierarchy carried certain obligations in his private life, a great responsibility indeed. Therefore, the main question was how to interpret the engagement of the prime minister's son with a person from a politically "wrong" family—since a

family was still an important feature of individual iden-
tity in Albania. In a country that prided itself on never
giving in to "enemy" bourgeois ideology, could this engage-
ment be a sign of liberalization? On the other hand, it
could be just the opposite, a sign of the weakness of the
class struggle, an error of judgment by the minister, per-
haps a, for him, fatal error.

After only a couple of weeks, however, the prime min-
ister had canceled the wedding. In doing so he demon-
strated that his loyalty to the party came first and to his
family only second. To admit his misjudgment in public
was no small thing to do, yet he thought that he would
thus save face. After all, he was the number two man in
power; this gesture should have meant something . . .

However, after a few months of speculation it became
obvious that the first secretary had decided to interpret
the engagement as a sign of weakness. The old Communist
should have known better than to give in to his son's desire
to marry into such a highly unsuitable family, it was ru-
mored to be said. He's become too soft, too bourgeois, it
was whispered. If he cannot control even his own son—
how is he supposed to lead the whole country one day?

The minister, indeed, seemingly had lost his grip on
power, because the essence of power is control.

A tragic love affair, Romeo and Juliet, some said after-
ward. But in Albania no one was preoccupied with what
happened to the youngsters. Should one indulge the feelings
of two youngsters when the security of the state could be

at stake? Was it worthwhile to make such a risky deci-sion? Surely the successor was aware of the problematic family when he approved the engagement? If he was not, it speaks even more against him as a future first secretary. The first secretary as a matter of principle should not trust anyone, not even his friends, much less a family with such suspect members. Rather, he should have fol-lowed good old Stalinist credo: Trust is good—but control is better.

It was also said that, although the first secretary—the minister's old comrade in arms and friend—was worried about such a development, he said nothing to him. The first secretary was so worried that he suggested a meeting of the Politburo. He decided that the Politburo should deal with this; it should present the problem of the prime min-ister and give him an opportunity for self-criticism. Surely he would come to his senses; this method always worked. And so the session was convened. As usual, such meetings went on for a few days. Just when the prime minister's turn came to speak, the meeting ended; it was supposed to continue the next day. Most probably, the first secretary would forgive his friend and successor, the boy would not marry the girl, and that would be it. But the next meeting did not take place. This was fatal for the minister . . .

Yet one cannot but wonder: Was it perhaps postponed in order to make it fatal?

That night, the night between the first and the second meetings, the minister committed suicide, or "suicide." It seems that he did not believe that the first secretary would forgive him. He knew his old comrade and friend better, he knew his cruelty—which had escalated with the attacks of acute paranoia he had been experiencing lately, apart from the diabetes and cerebral ischemia he was suffering from. I heard about it in conspiratorial tones from my colleague at the hospital who treated him—we all knew about his paranoia but were not allowed to mention it. The first secretary suffered from insomnia and hallucinations, apart from persecution mania, said my colleague, rather worried about the political consequences his mental state could have. He told me this just a month or so before the whole event—and voilà, there it is, the political consequence, a grand display of his sheer madness!

But then, again, there are people who love conspiracies, and they said something completely different: that the whole affair had been orchestrated. The engagement was only a pretext, a good motive for the first secretary to get rid of his main rival. In other words, it was an inner battle for power.

Therefore, a decision about his funeral must have been highly problematic: where to bury such a person—in the Martyrs' Cemetery or not? If yes, what was the message? If not, what was the message? Should it be a civilian funeral or not? So many questions . . . Previously, in a similar case of suicide by a Politburo member, the corpse was buried and exhumed five times! In the end, the minister was not given an official funeral; this status was indicated by the absence

of official speeches and any gunfire salute. After a while, his
body disappeared from his grave . . .

As a result of the whole sordid affair, not only the
prime minister but also his whole family was arrested
without any explanation. His wife and three sons were
imprisoned. One son committed suicide. He could not
stand torture, I heard. The mother died in prison, and the
two other sons are still serving a prison sentence.

In a note from 1985, Mother added that the investigators found two, not one, sheets of paper. One was a letter to his family and the other was a sheet inscribed with only two lines from an old Albanian folk song:

> *O ju korba qe me hani*
> *syte e zi mos mi ngani.*

> *[Oh, you ravens devouring me*
> *don't touch my black eyes]*

"It is not clear why this second sheet was not mentioned before," she commented. Or did it, in some way, point to the possibility that he had been forced into suicide? My mother, it seems, concluded that this definitely confirmed her suspicion of Raven's role in it all. By the way, on a separate sheet that she perhaps added to the notebook later on—she wrote in red pencil: *"I heard from a reliable source that an investigation was launched into his suicide. Allegedly, a man was seen entering the*

minister's house late that night. The official report states that his
face could not be recognized because of the heavy rain. It is only
known that a dark, tall man dressed in black left the house in the
early morning hours, walking hastily toward the city. 'His black
coat flew in the wind like the wings of a bird,' the report added."

My mother's only comment was an exclamation mark. My comment, however, is that it is not easy to believe that the writer of this report, based probably on an agent watching the house, perhaps even to ensure that the designated persona finished his task, would express himself in such poetic language. But evidently, in this country, poetry and fiction are more normal than news and information.

At the very end of her glued-in notebook there are only a few additional notes. In 1985 she wrote: "The first secretary is dead, finally." The other is from 1991, written in pencil again: "Today the two minister's sons were released from prison." And again, a couple of months later: "The first secretary's wife is in jail!" The last note is from November 19, 2001: "The remains of the minister found."

Of course, I understand that the reason my mother kept her diary in secrecy was because of the strange witness whose identity she kept to herself—but also because she mentioned the forbidden topic, the first secretary's illness. But it still fascinates me that she died believing that this secret should not be revealed, at least not during her lifetime. I understand that she had no strength left anymore. She feared for me, although I managed to stay in America, to her great joy as well as sorrow, because she could not see me more often.

You see, she lacked faith in democracy. I guess she was not alone; her whole generation did not trust any government at all. Perhaps with good reason. Never mind the political changes; there are still forces and people at work here that could have harmed her, perhaps even me. Indeed, many people in power are the same ones from before! Therefore, better to hush it up, she must have thought. Instead she kept a secret diary and never dared to even mention it to me, not even so many years after the fall of Communism in Albania. Especially not to me. Knowledge of any kind was a curse in our society. The more access to knowledge and information a person had, the more suspicious it was. Therefore, we had a ban on watching foreign TV shows or listening to foreign radio news programs.

She pulled all her strings to send me to America. She did it for a specific reason: Namely, even long after the first secretary's family had lost its power, she was still afraid of the possible consequences. She was insistent, although I was her only child and she was divorced. I resisted . . . stupid me! I was young, and my friends were the most important thing to me. I did not care as much about the future; they did not teach us to be ambitious. On the contrary, we learned that we didn't have to worry; the state would take care of us. And that it was normal to build some seven hundred thousand bunkers to protect us from an imaginary enemy.

As I told you, I am convinced that she must have known exactly who Raven was, perhaps she even knew him personally (he did not come to her for nothing), but she kept the identity of the person to herself. And his terrible secret as well. That event changed my mother's life and mine. The consequences for her were serious: She stopped believing in the leadership of the Communist Party and, moreover, in Communism as a system. She lost the comfort of thinking that Albanian Communism was just a matter of the wrong people in the wrong place—that the idea was right, only the practice was wrong.

The other day, during my mother's funeral, seeing her old friends, some of them also ghosts of times past (like the director of the hospital, a party strongman), I suddenly remembered one event. Just before I left for America in 1994 I had a meeting in the Daiti Hotel with a relative who was supposed to arrange for my visa. There I saw the younger son of the late first secretary. He had no real power, except for the power of his family name.

The son looked astonishingly like his father, tall and good-looking. Therefore, whenever he entered the Daiti Hotel, everybody looked at him a bit startled, even those who knew him well. As if the spirit of the dead patriarch was walking among them. Looking at him you suddenly found yourself in the company of a ghost. But was he a ghost, I wonder? At least, in 1994 the son was greeted with such reverence that I found it perplexing to see. Demonstrating reverence (born out of fear of his father) to this insignificant son, they bowed to the shadow of a man and his times—and not to the shadows of the thousands of people executed or dead in labor camps and prisons during his reign. So yes, in his presence people were reminded of his father, and this is how the late first secretary continued to live on for yet another generation. Reading my mother's diary, I wondered: How much longer will Albania live with its ghosts?

But on the other hand, my mother did not burn her diary,

though she could have done so. She had both the time and the opportunity, and I am sure she contemplated it. Today I take this as a good sign, a sign of faith in me, in the next generation. This is the reason why I brought the diary to you, to make it public in whatever form you see fit. It is about time!

AVAILABLE FROM PENGUIN

They Would Never Hurt a Fly
War Criminals on Trial in The Hague

Acclaimed novelist and journalist Slavenka Drakulić
writes about the people behind the crimes committed
during the most brutal conflict in Europe in the last
fifty years.

ISBN 978-0-14-303542-8

S.
A Novel about the Balkans

Set during the Bosnian war, *S.* is the story of a woman
who, through flashbacks, relives the unspeakable crimes
she has endured, and in doing so depicts the darkest side
of human nature during wartime.

Now a major motion picture titled *As If I Am Not There*

ISBN 978-0-14-029844-4

Café Europa
Life After Communism

In this brilliant work of political reportage,
Drakulić illustrates how Europe remains a divided
continent after the fall of the Berlin Wall.

ISBN 978-0-14-027772-2

PENGUIN
BOOKS